HUNTER MOON

The Witches of Langstone Bay

JOANNE MALLORY

Lighthouse Press
www.lighthousepress.co.uk

Hunter Moon
The Witches of Langstone Bay, Book 2

Copyright © Joanne Mallory
First published Oct, 2017
Second edition (revised) March, 2018.
Published by Lighthouse Press, March, 2018.

Lighthouse Press
www.lighthousepress.co.uk

Cover - Design by Studio 13

"The world is full of
magic things,
patiently waiting for our senses
to grow sharper."

- W.B. Yeats

CHAPTER 1

THE NAGGING PINGING of the seatbelt light sounded above her head.

Sleepily opening her eyes, Jess looked out of the plane window to see the Thames beneath her, winding through London. Straightening up as best as she could manage in the tiny seat, she stifled a yawn and checked her watch: 1.30pm.

They'd be on the tarmac at Heathrow within the next thirty minutes, but it would be gone three before she got her luggage and grabbed a cab across London, and that's only if the M4 was feeling cooperative.

She had to be at Tower Bridge for the gala dinner by 7.30pm.

Rapidly running through her mental checklist, she added in an hour at the museum, to check on the arrival of the artifact from Rome.

Rolling her eyes at her chances of getting everything done, she sighed and turned away from the window. The last thing she needed was to watch London rush up towards her.

The pressure in the cabin intensified as the plane began its descent.

Closing her eyes, she forced herself to relax back into her seat, and mentally cursed not being on the earlier flight, and having to go to the bloody gala in the first place...and anything else she could think of.

A smirk crossed her lips. She'd get Jason back for palming the gala into her lap. He knew she hated these things: all those people and cocktail conversation, all the hidden agendas, and the desire to increase their *networking* reach. She quelled a mock shudder at just the thought of it. Oh yeah, she'd get him back alright.

The wheels touched the runway with a small double bump, and she released a breath. Being a passenger just didn't work for her.

Standing in the aisle, Jess tucked her dark hair behind her ear. In a plea for patience, she began mentally counting as she eyed the woman at the front of the queue. The woman had got her hand luggage stuck on the overhead door, and instead of moving into the now empty row of seats in front of her so that people could get off, she'd decided to block the aisle while the flight attendant was trying to unhook it.

Despite being asked to move by several passengers, she continued to stand there, huffing that people "shouldn't be so impatient."

The tempers of the passengers were rising, and Jess took in a slow breath and pushed energy out from her center, creating an intangible barrier, defending herself from the waves of negative energy that flooded the cabin; she didn't need to be soaking that up.

Looking down at her watch, she frowned: 2.15pm. She could do with being off this plane and away from the thrum. Staring at the offending piece of luggage, she muttered a release spell beneath her breath.

The hinge on the overhead door gave way with a clatter,

barely missing the over-tired flight attendant as it thudded onto the seat, and the bag fell into the aisle.

Rolling her eyes, Jess looked up. She really needed more time and focus when it came to spell-work.

As the woman faffed about with her luggage, the man behind her finally gave up and pushed past, and the queue began to edge slowly forward.

As she approached the flight attendant, Jess lightly touched her shoulder, passing her a little energy boost. "Are you alright? That came down with some force."

The petite blonde offered Jess a warm smile, the tight lines around her eyes easing away as her tiredness abated. "Oh, don't worry about me. I'm all finished for a few days."

Smiling at her, Jess shuffled off the plane. Guiltily sliding her hands into her pockets, she made a mental note to add 'release spells' to the ever-growing list of things that she should work on.

Pulling the soft leather strap of her messenger handbag over her head, she adjusted it across her body, and weaved her way through the crowds. The wheels of her neat suitcase made a pleasing rhythmical sound as she strolled from baggage claim across the packed airport.

As she approached the vast row of automatic doors, bitterly cold air raced across the tiles, whipping round her ankles. Rome may have only been a couple of hours ago, but it had been a balmy 28 degrees—while London was ranking high on the grey, wet and freezing-o-meter.

They'd been in the throes of a heatwave before she'd left, and she'd only been gone for two weeks. What was with this weather? When had the summer gone on hiatus?

Adding the moan to her already pissy mood, she headed for the line of taxis, nodding her thanks at the driver when he opened his boot, and reached to take her case from her.

Settling into the back of the cab, Jess lightly cleared her throat, before asking for Exhibition Road.

She pulled her phone from her pocket as the cab eased into the traffic. It had switched over to an Italian phone provider a few days ago, and for reasons unknown to her had stopped receiving, so she'd been cut off from the rest of the world. If only it had frazzled out before getting that one last message... Opening her texts she re-read it.

Having to fly to Ireland, can you take my place at the gala dinner? Left tickets with front desk. See you when you're back from down south. Jason :)

The rain was pounding against the taxi roof, hitting the windscreen with heavy splats, and Jess couldn't think of anything worse than having to drag out heels and slap on a smile.

One more week and she was officially on holiday for three glorious weeks.

And she was going home. Going to surprise her sister, and hope her brother might even be in the vicinity. She was planning on dragging them to the pub, sitting on the beach, and seeing what trouble she could entice her brother's Labrador, Murphy, to get in to.

It had been too long since they'd all been together.

Finding them firmly in her thoughts, she let her mind drift, until she could gently detect their energies. Happy that everything felt okay, she stared back down at her phone; still no signs of picking up a signal, she couldn't even text them.

With a sigh, she blinked dry eyes at the too bright phone screen. Shutting it down, she dropped it in her pocket— getting it sorted would be tomorrow's job.

Jess turned to stare out of the window and looked at the westbound traffic heading out of the city; it was gridlocked.

She supposed she should be grateful that she had this bloody do to go to tonight. Or else she'd most likely be sitting on a gridlocked M25 as well.

Huffing under her breath, she rolled her eyes at the thought. She wouldn't care if she sat in traffic all night if she could get out of going to this gala.

Pointing at the plain gated entrance, she caught the driver's eye in the rear-view mirror. "Just here is fine."

The wet wind blasted her as she lifted her small suitcase, and raced round the taxi, swiping her ID card in the entrance panel. She was glad of the looming museum, shielding her from the worst of the weather as she pushed through the door to the staff entrance.

The warmly lit reception was a haven from the chaotic wind.

Jess clicked the door shut behind her, grappling with her hair, and blowing it from her eyes she came face-to-face with a laughing Steve.

"Miss Jess! Fine weather, if you're a duck." His bright blue eyes sparkled, as he clasped his hands over the desk and grinned at her. "How was Rome?"

Heading over and leaning on the reception desk, she wiped the last remaining droplets of rain from her face. "It was a heck of a lot warmer than this. What's happened to our summer, Steve?"

Briefly smoothing back his silver hair, he shrugged, spreading his hands wide. "Don't you worry, Miss Jess, it's just a quick storm to release the heat, I'd say. I had a call from Jason. Understand I have to pass some tickets your way?" He raised his brows at her, pulling two tickets from the drawer, holding them towards her.

Pinching one of them from his grasp, she read it. "This is it, for tonight's gala. Who's the other ticket for?"

Smiling, Steve looked over her shoulder. "Ah, perfect

timing." Placing his clipboard on the desk, Steve busied himself updating his records, as a slight cough behind her had her turning around.

Jess faced the smiling, hoodie-wearing man coming towards her.

"I'm Sebastian. Glad you got back in time."

He held out his hand, and Jess looked at it, before looking back up at him. "Sebastian?"

"Um, sure."

His hand remained between them.

Shaking herself, she offered him a quick smile. "Sorry, still a bit frazzled from the flight and all. Nice to meet you." Sliding her hand firmly into his, her eyes widened as a little frisson of energy travelled up her arm. Her smile lifted into a smirk as she held his hand for a fraction longer than necessary, enjoying the buzz.

How interesting.

Reaching behind her, she grabbed the second ticket from the desk. "So this is yours?"

His dark hair had clearly been pulled through his fingers too many times today. She looked into his warm brown eyes, bright with intelligence and laughter. His grey hoodie was spattered with rain marks. Dark jeans encased solid thighs, and a day's worth of stubble gave him a relaxed look.

But the Cartier diving watch wrapped round his wrist, and the expensive, but well-worn walking boots hinted that he had some very interesting pastimes.

He, most definitely, was a picture.

Jess held the ticket towards him as she studied him; a touch of mischief lit his eyes as he held her gaze.

"I'm afraid so. I believe Jason is hoping I'll take over some of these god-awful functions from him, and he said you're the expert to walk me through the dos and don'ts." Sliding the ticket into his back pocket, he shrugged. "I gotta warn you though, I'm crap at the meeting and the greeting."

Briefly acknowledging that she'd now be making more of an effort with her own attire for tonight, she nodded at his jeans. "Duly noted. But you do have a suit, right?"

His laugh was deep and easy, and she found herself smiling at the rich sound.

"Sure—don't get me wrong, black tie would be a stretch. But a suit, I can manage."

"Okay then." Turning to Steve, she gestured to the clock. "Can you sort out a car to collect us both? Get me last at 7.15."

"Sure thing, Miss Jess."

Grabbing the door, she threw him a smile. "Thanks, Steve. Oh, has a delivery come for me?"

Looking at her, Steve's white head bobbed in acknowledgment as he gestured at Sebastian with his biro.

Sliding past her through the door she was holding open, Sebastian waited in the empty corridor.

"I signed for it this morning."

The scent of the rain lifted from him as he passed her, the wind had clearly blown him about too.

Not used to feeling short, she mentally added 'taller heels' to tonight's dress code.

"Oh great, thanks." She fell into step beside him as they headed for the storage department, curious as to why Jason hadn't mentioned they had a newbie on the team.

"So, have you been here long?" *What. The. Hell?* Jess gritted her teeth at the ridiculous words that had just fallen from her lips. Why hadn't she just asked him if he came here often?

"Technically, I'm not actually *here*."

Looking him up and down, she lifted her brows at him. "No? Could've fooled me."

He pushed his hands into the pockets of jeans as they

walked. The long hallway ran the entire length of the museum; gothic arched windows lined the walls, taking the brunt of the rain.

His lips lifted in a slight smile, and as she studied the shadow dusting his jaw, she wondered what time he'd arrived this morning. What could Jason possibly be up to?

"I don't officially start until next week. So I've got a few days to find my feet before you go on holiday."

"Uh-huh." Her brow arched as she looked at him. *Curiouser and curiouser.* "And I suppose Jase flying off to Ireland has thrown you in the deep end?"

He shrugged. "I'm sure I'll manage." Swiping his security card, he held the door for her.

Riffling through the pile of clipboards, he pulled one out, handing it over. "It arrived by courier. I thought you'd want to open and check it yourself."

Taking the board, she read the delivery note. She had to give him a tick in the box for professional etiquette; it narked her something rotten when her stuff got interfered with. Not that the artifacts were *hers*, but that wasn't the point. Putting a halt to her mind's crazy rambling, she murmured her thanks, noting the aisle number.

She could feel the expectation pouring from him, but he merely gave her a polite smile and walked away, leaving her to it.

Stopping at the door, he turned back. "I'll see you later, then?"

She raised her brows in question, giving him a smile. "Don't you want to have a look?"

A grin split his face, heavy dark lashes swept down as he gave her a deliberate nod, purposefully coming towards her. "You betcha! I love a good libation bowl. But I didn't want to interfere, you know? Drives me mad when people go rummaging through my artifacts."

Releasing a pent up breath, she gave a relieved laugh. "I do know. I know exactly what you mean." Heading down the aisles of storage boxes and crates, she grabbed an abandoned trolley, while he traced the box numbers until he found hers.

He lifted the packing crate down onto the flatbed trolley and waited beside her.

She could tell he was barely restraining himself from rubbing his hands together with glee, and she couldn't help but smile. She felt the same. Each new find gave bigger glimpses of the past, filled more gaps in her knowledge.

Snipping the straps, she levered off the lid. She could feel the hum from the bowl already reaching her palms as she carefully eased the packaging aside.

His head bowed close to her as they both leant over the crate, and she heard his breath catch in his throat as he waited. Excitement trickled along his skin, reverberating against her, and the wintery scent of him held hints of the sea.

He'd pulled up the sleeves of his hoodie as he reached into the crate, holding back the straw-like packing as she moved it.

His forearms were tanned, dusted with dark hair and strong. Each muscle flexed as he carefully helped her. She found herself 'accidentally' brushing his fingers as she freed the large bowl.

The hammered silver pounded with so much energy, it still surprised her that others couldn't feel it.

Lifting it from the confines, she held it out to him.

His eyes widened as he traced the engraved chariots. "That's beautiful." His hushed whisper brushed across her, tickling her nerve endings.

She watched his fingertip trace the filigree markings, catching her breath at the sudden buzz of desire that shot through her.

Heavy silence filled the air as he studied the bowl, and she studied him. His brows furrowed as he took in every mark, as his fingers searched for signs of use and age. His full lips parted, revealing the edge of straight white teeth, his tongue caught between them as he concentrated.

Lifting his gaze to clash with hers, heat flooded her face at being caught staring at him. He stood silently facing her, and she unconsciously lowered the bowl, her gaze locked with his, her breath coming in shallow pants.

She had no idea what to say, or how to break the intense current running between them, as he cautiously took a step closer.

His hands joined her own on the bowl, the ancient silver clasped between them as they faced each other.

The sharp clatter of noise from the next aisle had her jerking away from him, like a teenager who'd been sprung, and the bowl slipped from her fingertips heading for the concrete.

Their fumbled scrabbling saved it from hitting the hard floor; a nervous laugh breathlessly escaped him, as he looked up at her from his bent position, the bowl clutched to his chest.

Jess held both palms against her pounding heart, a smile slowly creeping up on her as she stared down him, shaking her head. "Phew. Good catch."

Coming to his full height, he patted the bowl. "Tell me about it." His expression teasing as he raised a brow at her. "I got a bit distracted there for a minute."

Heat flooded her system, rushing back to her face as she took the bowl he now held out to her. Tilting her head, she let her hair hide her from him as she placed the bowl back in the crate.

Ugh, he was funny too. Dammit; fit, fine and funny. Dammit-bloody-dammit.

Giving herself an inner shake, she sealed the box back up, busying herself with completing the documentation.

"How did you convince them to let us have it?"

Signing her signature, she collected the box, sliding it back on the shelf, using it as an excuse to move away from him. "No such luck. They're just lending, for the Gods and Worship Exhibition in October, then the *Museo di Roma* will be wanting her back."

Feeling like she had herself under slightly tighter control, she gathered up the paperwork. She'd have to have her wits about her when it came to dealing with him; a little flirting was good for the soul, but he was potent stuff.

"Come on." Turning back, she grinned, waving him to her. "You've got a suit to shake out, and time is ticking."

Shutting the door with a foul glare at the now pouring rain, she and her luggage made for the elevator to take them up to her flat. The building was a mix of VIP and employee accommodation provided by the Museum, and after being stuck for three years in the basement flat, she'd finally managed to snag a gorgeous little slice of heaven, three floors up that overlooked the private garden.

Turning the key, she pushed open the front door, before stepping inside. She left the suitcase in the little hallway and walking through her apartment began turning on the lights.

She headed for the bedroom, and opened the floor to ceiling fitted Victorian wardrobe doors, and stared in at work suits and neat, sensible, black, *work suitable* cocktail dresses. And that was the only problem with this place; other than a couple of pairs of jeans, she kept it kitted out for work.

And that just wouldn't do. Not tonight.

Catching her reflection in her dresser mirror, she stopped. Her long dark hair was a windblown mess, but what had been tired brown eyes now held a glint of excitement, at the prospect of having a flirtatious evening, with the charmer that Jason had left her to babysit. She'd find out what his motives were later—and damn well get her own back. But for now, she hadn't had a little fun in far too long.

"Time to get my act together." She had just shy of two hours, and she'd had enough of the dark-grey afternoon for a start. Rushing round she drew curtains and turned on lights, liking the nice peachy glow that warmed everything up.

Spying the speaker across the room, she pulled magic from her core, and with a point of her finger, sent a buzz towards it, requesting music pour out. She grinned. It had been six years ago when magic had all but tossed her from her bed, and every little aspect of it still filled her with pleasure.

Drifting towards her en-suite, the music followed her, the flush-ceiling-lights reflected from all the glass and silver, and the mirrors reflected the travertine tiles. This room had been dire when she'd moved in; she would've rather washed in a bucket on the roof. But Jason and her brother had helped her to work wonders.

She played about with soaps and shampoo bottles, lining everything up the way she liked it, before turning on the shower, letting the room fill with steam.

The hot spray washed away the last of the flight and the unseasonably wet and grey day.

Wrestling her waist-length hair up onto her head, she lathered it up, softly singing.

She wondered what had been so important that Jason had needed to rush off to Ireland for, and she couldn't believe for a minute that he was going to cut down on attending all the functions and events. She snorted at the thought. "That would put a serious dent in his extracurriculars." She smirked to herself at her own joke. She'd be sure to text him that when her phone was back in action.

She rinsed out the conditioner, before shutting off the shower.

Jess grabbed a towel and padded back to her bedroom, drying the last errant droplets from her skin as she went. Bending from the waist, she flipped her hair forward and wrapped it up in the towel, eyeing the wardrobe as she did so.

Lightly biting her lip, she headed for her dresser. Opening the drawer, she looked in at the small amount of supplies she kept here, and selected two violet candles, and a piece of ribbon the same color, to amplify energy.

Standing in front of the south facing mirror she placed the tapered candles in plain ceramic holders, and lightly wrapping her hands around the wicks, she closed her eyes and felt the flame rise from within her. Felt the magic trickle through her veins and settle in her palms, sparking the candles alight.

The dual flames burnt high for just a brief flash of time, bathing her skin in the ancient energy that danced all around. Whispering thanks she lifted the candles and placed them on the floor, either side of the tall wardrobe doors, before taking the violet ribbon and wrapping it around the two crystal doorknobs, before tying a loose knot.

Lifting her palms, magic hazed, trickling a lilac spark across the engraved wood.

Whispering beneath her breath, she chanted the spell times three.

> "From here to there,
> No distance will be,
> As I open these doors,
> So Mote It Be."

The candles sparked and flickered at her feet, as the energy pounded between her palms and the doors, before the flames finally hissed out.

Clenching her hands to fists, she waited a heartbeat

before opening her palms, releasing the remnant power, offering it up to the ether, before untying the ribbon.

Holding the crystal doorknobs, she slowly pulled the doors wide, to find herself looking into her wardrobe that was back home, in the bay. Rolling her eyes, she grinned. "Goddess, yes."

She ran a fleeting hand across the coat hangers and selected her favorite dress. A simple black shift that fitted like a dream, with a halter neckline that did wonders for her. The back and wrist-length sleeves were black and completely sheer, and she loved it.

Rummaging through far too many shoeboxes, she came up with her cherished suede pumps with a wicked heel and a dainty ankle strap.

Sitting back on the carpet, she crossed her legs, still smiling to herself as she closed the doors.

Pressing her palms flat against the wood, she closed her eyes, and waited for her energy to focus and still, before clearly stating, "Reverse."

A chill wind blew across her bare skin, and she felt the shift as everything returned to normal.

Well, mostly normal; the shoe box sat next to her, and her dress lay across her bare legs.

"Time to get motivating, woman."

Pushing to her feet, she caught her reflection in the mirror; lavender flecks still shimmered in her eyes and the hazey magic was slowly fading.

She smiled to herself as she laid the clothes on her bed, before attacking the towel on her head, shaking out her wet hair.

Forty minutes. She had forty minutes! She applied a little makeup, a little lotion and a little perfume, all in-between bouts of giving her hair a cool blow dry, and smoothing on lacy shorts and thigh highs. Tucking the lace and silks back into her lingerie drawer, she acknowledged the madness of owning what seemed like the entire Agent Provocateur collection. But she loved it. Did anyone ever get to see? No. But that wasn't the point. *She* liked it, and that was good enough for her.

Nearly strangling herself trying to do up the zip on her dress without catching her skin or her hair, Jess wondered if these designers thought women were contortionists?

Gathering her hair over her shoulder, she deftly wrapped it into a side chignon, securing it with bobby pins, before finally sitting on the edge of the bed, to slip on and fasten the buckles of her favorite Alexander McQueens.

She grabbed her little black clutch, throwing in a lipstick and her bank cards.

Picking her phone up off the side, she headed for the window, pulling back the curtain to see if the car had arrived, before checking her phone. It was still flashing a 'No Carrier' message. Tossing it on the coffee table as she passed, she picked up her door keys and went down for the car.

CHAPTER 2

THE ELEGANT BLACK Mercedes sat at the curb, its tinted windows shining as the rain streaked down them. The crisply dressed chauffeur approached with his black umbrella, sheltering her from the weather as he accompanied her to the car.

She loved this bit. All the strangers and shop-talk bored her senseless, but if the whole evening was nothing more than her being chauffeur-driven in circles around London and dropped off back here she'd be ecstatic. The getting ready and being escorted to a fine automobile—she loved the show of it all.

But then, tonight was different. Behind the dark glossy window sat a man. A man who'd stunned her senses, and that didn't happen very often. Unless she took a trip down memory lane to her uni years, it hadn't happened at all.

She held her breath as the door was opened. Trying to be as ladylike as possible as she turned and lowered herself onto the fine leather, lifting her legs in to the cozy warmth.

Readying a smile she turned, to find the seat next to her empty. Jess huffed as disappointment dropped through her. It looked like tonight was going to be a total washout after all.

"Ma'am, Mr Hunter has asked me to inform you that he'll meet you at the Tower."

Lightly clearing her throat, she offered what she hoped was a nonchalant tone. "Oh, fine."

She knew she'd failed miserably as the polite chauffeur's lips twitched in the mirror.

Buggering-dammit.

She scrunched her face-up nastily at her own reflection in the window, and turned back to the chauffeur. "Was there a problem?"

"I don't believe so, Ma'am."

Almost grinning at him, she leant back in her seat. *Bloody men.* She watched the rain hit the panoramic roof, as the grey clouds above London hid the sun and streamed over her head. The scent of the rain eased in through the air-con, and she could just detect a hint of the Thames before it came into view, and the glorious Tower Bridge rising above it.

Allowing herself to be escorted from the car by the highly amused chauffeur, he left her safely inside the dry entrance, to ascend the Victorian staircase that curled ever upwards, the wet air racing up the stairs after her.

The din from the Gala above reached her, and she took a steadying breath as she came to the viewing deck. Circular tables were laid with white linen and polished cutlery, and the windows and glass walkway let in views of the whole of London. Gods, she loved this city.

Removing her ticket from her clutch to give to the approaching maître d', the tingle reached her just before a warm hand clasped her elbow. Keeping her eyes forward, she let a little smile tip her lips.

"Sebastian. You're late."

Reaching out, he slid the ticket from her fingers, handing them to the *maître d'*, who turned to guide them to their table. "I'd like to apologize for not arriving with you."

Taking the seat that was offered, she smiled politely and turned to face him as he sat. His dark grey suit fitted perfectly, and the light blue tie sat beautifully against his softer blue silk shirt. He looked delicious.

Raising her brows at his flawless manners, she grinned at him. "No biggy. You were only a couple of minutes behind."

Despite his polished appearance, she could feel frenetic energy pouring from him. He'd tamed his hair, but she could tell he itched to run his fingers through it. She stifled a smirk; she wouldn't mind running her fingers through it either. He'd looked good earlier, in a rough jeans and boots sort of way, but the suit fitted him perfectly. He was bigger, just all over bigger, than she'd thought, and she liked the constant buzz of excitement she got from just looking at him.

Shaking his head, Seb chuckled. The husky sound made her smile.

"Well, anyway, I'm sorry." Easing back in his seat, he made room for the waiter, who leant over to pour their wine. "So, what's the deal with these shindigs? And why do I feel like we've drawn the short straw, and Jason is off somewhere having more fun than we're about to?"

His voice was like his laugh, deep and soft, and every guest that passed by dragged his scent across to her, his after-shave somehow reminding her of the sea. The tan on his skin declared that, unlike her, he hadn't spent most of the summer in draughty archives. In fact, he was proving more delightful by the second.

Casting her eye across their currently empty table she read the name plates. "Oh, Jason has left us without a paddle, that's for sure." Nodding at them, she picked up her wine glass, taking a healthy sip of the citrusy white. "This motley crew are all private employees: two buyers, a dealer, and a collector. They'll be boring as hell. The idea of tonight was so that we could introduce ourselves to the new head of department for the Native American section at the Smithsonian."

As he picked up his own glass, his hand looked too big for the fine crystal. He was starting to relax, his energy field settling down, not bouncing jerkily against hers. She watched as his shoulders lost some of their tension and he released a pent up breath, before giving her a knowing look.

"And I take it they're not here?"

She shook her head. "Nope. The waiter was removing their place-settings from the front table as I came in."

Casting his gaze across the truly spectacular view, he looked at her before glancing down at his feet, and murmured, "Well, there are worse places to have dinner."

Following his gaze, his tan brogues looked almost super-imposed as the glass floor dropped away to the road below where the traffic flowed one way, the Thames the other.

"You're not afraid of heights, then?" She raised her brows questioningly, meeting his gaze square on, and felt the chemistry crackle between them.

His brown eyes held hers for a fraction longer than necessary, and she enjoyed the lustful current that tripped through her.

"Not afraid of anything much. What about you?"

Leaning back, she crossed her legs beneath the table, and shrugged. "Not really. I'm not keen on earwigs, if that helps?"

His nose wrinkled at the thought, and he closed his mouth on whatever he'd been going to say, smoothing out his expression as two of their table-mates arrived.

Jess gave her hellos and introduced Sebastian, giving him a knowing look as Matilda launched into her thoughts on the latest government arts cuts, before her backside had even hit the chair.

As the main course was cleared his eyes had all but glazed over. Jess felt pretty much the same. Matilda's phone trilled inside her bag, and as she frantically rummaged for it, Jess slid a long look his way, before addressing the table. "Excuse us, won't you? I'm just going to give Sebastian a look at some of the amazing moldings before the final course is served." He rose with her as she spoke, giving the table in general a polite smile.

Weaving their way between the tables until they reached what would soon be the dance floor, she leant on the window railing and looked across London, heaving a sigh. "It's going to be a long night. We've still got pudding and coffees to go."

"Tell me about it. There was no whisky on the menu either."

"Now that really is a crime." She laughed as he shook his head. The last of the cloud was passing over, and the blue sky framed him. It was as if time had thrown him forward, he had an air of the old-fashioned aristocrat about him.

"Of course, if the people we're here to meet aren't actually here..." His voice trailed away as he looked innocently at her, his dark eyes full of mischief and fun.

Planting a serious expression on her face, she nodded. "I'm sure the museum has some historical emergency that needs our attention..."

He leant towards her, warmth radiating from him, as his lips barely brushed her ear. Shivers raced up her spine, and she held wholly still as he whispered, "Forget coffee. I know a great whisky bar, right close to here."

She inwardly groaned at how his fabulous scent filled her senses, how his heated breath caused goose bumps... She was seriously going to have to get a grip on her suddenly active libido.

But then, willpower never had been her strong point. "Let's get out of here."

Laughing, he surprised her by grabbing her hand, pulling her towards the door, and offering an excuse to the passing waiter. He took the inside on the spiraling staircase, his warm, rough palm, firmly engulfing her hand as he steadied her descent.

As they stepped from the Tower, Jess looked skyward. A late summer wind had blown away the last of the rain, leaving a warm, damp night.

"So," he prompted her, "you were talking about earwigs."

He kept hold of her hand, as he steered her right, and they walked towards the Thames.

"Sure. Hate 'em. Not frightened. Just think they're a bit gross. Is it Sebastian or Seb?"

He nodded, briefly looking down at her. "Seb, mostly."

Stealing furtive glances at him as they walked, she studied him. She wasn't small, and with a little help from four inch heels, she never found height an issue. But he still had a few inches on her, and his hand had virtually swallowed hers. What did he eat, for gods' sake?

"What about you? Is it Jess or Jessica?"

"Depends. I'm Jess, unless you count my brother. Then it's full on Jessica. Or Steve at the Museum, he calls me 'Miss Jess', and I always feel like I've stepped onto the lanai of some country house in the Deep South."

He gave a short burst of laugher, turning smiling brown eyes on her. "Yeah, I noticed that today. Not bad for a guy from the East End of London."

She laughed. "I know, right. Probably left over from a past life."

He gave her a quizzical look that she merely shrugged off; she'd never seen any reason to pretend to be anything she wasn't. She wasn't about to run around sky-clad, shouting pagan chants either, but they were going to be working together, and he may as well get used to her.

She'd better remember that too; they *were* going to be working together, and here she was leaning into him like they

21

were on a date. Hating her own common sense, she sadly let go of his hand, inanely fiddling with her hair to cover it. "Where is this place then? I suppose one drink wouldn't hurt?"

Gesturing ahead, he slid the hand that had been holding hers in his pocket. "One? After half an hour with the art buyer I'm going to need a couple."

The sun was making her last effort of the day. The sky was mottled with purples and peaches as she burnt through the last remaining rainclouds, and Jess could see the steam beginning to rise from the pavement and rooftops as the rain evaporated.

He'd slowed his stride so she wasn't having to race to keep up with him. He even walked well. She hid a sad shake of her head at her bad luck. They had such good chemistry, but he was more than likely to be taking the empty office across the hall from her, and it just wouldn't do for them to be getting all tangled up.

Coming to a stop at a neat row of classic town houses, he led them towards the furthest one. The glossed, walnut front door sat back between its two ornate white columns. His hand came to rest on her lower back as he guided her up the three marble steps and lightly knocked the door.

She barely hid her surprise when he gave Jason's name.

The 'house' was clearly not a home.

As he led her up the stairs, the rooms they passed were set for dinner, some of the tables occupied, some not, and if the smell was anything to go by, the food must be amazing.

It was turning out to be quite a night.

The top floor opened out into a long, highly polished bar. Every single whisky known to man must have been perfectly placed on the mirrored back wall.

Leaning against the bar, he grinned at her, obviously feeling very pleased with himself. "What would you like?"

Laying her clutch on the bar top, she raised her brows and slowly enunciated her words. "Jason brought you here?"

He nodded at her. "Sure, he has membership, so does the museu—" His face took on a slightly awkward expression. "You didn't know that..."

The barman came to a stop before them. "On Mr MacIntyre's tab, Sir?"

Catching his eye, she gave him a sickly sweet smile, "Oh, I think so. He's such a dear, after all..." Pausing a beat, she glanced back at Seb. "I'll have the Balvenie 30. A large one."

His lips firmed to hold back the smile, as he nodded. "Two of those, please."

Following him, her eyes widened again at the pretty little rooftop garden, with intimate tables and candles already flickering as they waited for sunset. It was all framed against the back drop of the Thames, with the Tower of London spreading out on the other side of the water.

Easing herself into a plush seat deep with cushions, she held her silence until the waiter moved away.

"I'm going to bloody kill him." She frowned at Seb's easy grin. "He knows how I feel about whisky."

Making a nondescript noise in the back of his throat, his eyes sparkled with glee. "Well," he raised his heavily cut crystal tumbler towards her, "we'll get our own back sat right here." His voice was low and smooth, as if he were working through each syllable. "You know, nice and civilized."

Unable to hide her delighted smile, she slitted her eyes at him as she picked up her glass. "I like that."

Lightly tapping her glass with his, the clear sound bounced between them as she took her first sip.

The honeyed warmth hit her tongue as she swallowed, and she let a small breath leave her lips as it sank through her. "And a delicious revenge it will be."

Laughing around his own mouthful, he rolled his shoulders as the sun's rays just peeked over the rooftops, hitting his back and warming her face.

Propping his elbows on the table, he held his glass loosely in his grasp. "You know, whisky is a funny thing, it has a way of grabbing your memories. Like you—how come the Balvenie was your first choice?"

Leaning forward, she mirrored his pose. The sun streaked his hair, catching the caramel strands, and he absently pulled on his tie, loosening it.

"My brother, Adam. It's his favorite, and although it's not my favorite, I somehow always start with his."

Jess laughed softly, thinking of her stubborn brother. "He has his moments." Smiling into her glass, she took another sip, and focusing her magic, she sent Adam an intangible sisterly-poke, grinning when she felt the same in return. "But it's been me, him and my sister since my grandmother died, so we're pretty tight." He was still pulling at his tie, easing it a little lower, and she gestured at it with her glass. "If it's driving you mad, why don't you take it off? Unless there's a dress code in here?"

"I think it's a little smarter than no shirt, no shoes, no service. But I reckon I'll be alright without my tie." Coming to his feet, his frame blocked out the sun, his shadow falling across her as he took off his jacket. The shirt pulled across his chest, and she swallowed at the sudden dryness in her throat. His scent rushed across her: sun-warmed skin, aftershave and a hint of whisky.

He must work out—a lot. Dropping the jacket on the back of his chair, he pulled off the tie, and it was all Jess could do not to ask him to continue the show.

Then he grabbed his glass and came round to her side of the table.

"Budge up."

Easing down into the sea of cushions with her, he

propped his feet onto his now empty chair, crossing them at the ankles.

"I suppose 'take your tie off' does translate to 'make yourself comfortable'."

"It does in my book. Besides, there's nobody up here but us."

Shrugging, she unsnapped the ankle straps. Leaving her shoes on the floor, she curled her legs underneath her, facing him. "So, what about you? What's your favorite whisky and why?"

Holding his glass resting against the flat plains of stomach, he looked at her. "How badly are we punishing Jason?"

Not bothering to suppress her evil smile, she looked over, signaling the waiter.

"Ma'am?"

Handing over to Seb, she held her palms wide. "Have at it."

The look in his eyes was nothing short of wicked. "If you don't mind, we'll have two of the Glenmorangie 1983—large ones."

Pushing his empty glass onto the table, he grinned. "I'll be topping up the tab for this one."

She shook her head. "Nu-uh. Jason's gotta learn." Looking at him with interest, she leant her elbow on the back of the chair, her hand cupping her head. "You don't act like he's your boss. I know I don't either. But why don't you?"

"Me? I've known Jase for years. He's been trying to entice me away from McGill University ever since I started."

"McGill... That's Canada. How did he convince you? That's a gorgeous part of the world."

His brown eyes shadowed as she spoke, and she felt the tension tease back into him.

"The winters are rough, and I was in the mood for a change."

Letting the brief explanation slide, she nodded her thanks as the waiter approached, setting their

drinks down on the table.

The amber liquid reflected around the glasses as they both watched them.

"The Glenmorangie 1983—so what's the story?"

~

HE HAD SO many stories for this whisky. He looked over at her, readying himself to pick something short and funny, but her wide brown eyes were bright and questioning, and her beautifully full, soft lips pursed as she waited for him to answer.

Her soft honeysuckle scent kept bombarding his senses, and he found himself telling her the truth.

"My Dad bought two bottles when it was distilled in 1983, the year I was born. One for my eighteenth, the other for my twenty-first. The first we drank together."

Her gaze became very solemn, and she nodded, and shifting her legs from under her she sat up straight, collecting their glasses.

"In that case, we better do him justice."

Holding his glass out towards him, she waited, and he pushed up from his prone position. Taking the glass, his fingers brushed hers, and again he felt that tingle, the same as this afternoon.

Lifting her glass slightly, the sun sparkled around the crystal. "To your Dad."

Touching his glass to hers, he nodded. "He was a good man."

The taste hit him like a blast. He'd celebrated some of his darkest and brightest moments with this whisky, and now he was sharing it with her.

Her eyes softly closed as she sipped, the whisky still glistened on her lips, and, unable to stop himself, he leaned forward, catching the sip in a kiss.

Her small intake of breath was lost as his hand cupped her chin, and his tongue swept across, taking the last drops with her own dewy taste, before pulling back.

She drew in a soft breath, her eyes still closed as a smile brushed across her face, then her eyes opened and she raised her brows in question.

"He also said, never miss the chance to kiss a beautiful woman."

On a gurgle of laughter, she curled back into the cushions. "Did he, now? Well, I imagine you do him proud then."

Settling back down beside her his grin took on an untamed edge. "Me? Nah. Work keeps me too busy."

Taking another sip of the splendid whisky, he let the heat slide down his throat as she watched him.

"Hmm. I'll bet. But I tell you; if it didn't before, it will now. We've got a lot coming up as we move into the autumn calendar."

He let the velvety richness of her voice surround him as she talked about the artifacts coming up for display in the winter. Her full lips were a deep, perfect red, but soft. They shaped the words as she spoke, her tongue occasionally touching her neat white teeth. The sun had lost its glare as it slowly dropped below the roof of the opposite building, its final rays touching her hair. The elegant twist she'd artfully arranged showed off her heart shaped face, and her dark hair matched her chocolatey brown eyes. They were wide and full of laughter.

Long lashes fanned her face as she blinked, and her smile revealed slight dimples. The diamonds in her ears perfectly suited her; she oozed class, and he was thoroughly enjoying being swept along.

He'd been back in the UK for a couple of weeks, and the last few months in Canada seemed like another lifetime; someone else's lifetime.

He let his eyes drop to half-mast, and thoughts of Canada fell away as he allowed himself to enjoy watching her.

The silky nylon whispered across her legs as she moved, the fabric of the dress had a slight shimmer as it stretched to accommodate her thighs as she uncurled her legs, propping dainty feet alongside his on the chair.

Six months ago, he wouldn't have considered the nightmare situation of starting something with a colleague. But things changed, and he was more aware than ever, that life was too sodding short.

"I'm off to Cologne in October to review a collection for next spring. Where has Jase got you jetting off to?"

Lightly arching his back, he raised his brows at her. "Nowhere yet. I've been a few years here, there and everywhere, and I'm looking to steer clear of airports and departure lounges for a while.

Do you travel a lot?"

"Not really." She smoothly swirled the contents of her glass. "A couple of times a year, to view a big collection that we're looking to host." She gave a noncommittal shrug as she gazed across the roof-tops. "Or the occasional stop-over if there's something really special that Jason thinks we need to assess." Taking a last sip, she turned to him. The whisky had brought a warm flush across her cheekbones, and a relaxed sparkle to her gaze.

"The sun's going down."

He nodded. "So it is. Fancy a walk?"

He knew what she was thinking, watched the fleeting disappointment whisper in her eyes as she looked at him; knew she was readying herself to make *the* speech. A speech he'd made before, about how they worked together, and *it wouldn't be a good idea...*

"I'm staying at The Rembrandt till I find somewhere. You're close by, aren't you?"

A slight smile tipped her mouth. "Hmmm, literally right behind the hotel, on Alexander Square."

Coming to his feet he kept his back to her as he reached for his jacket, hiding his lustful smirk. "I may as well walk you home then.

CHAPTER 3

SHE MUST BE BLOODY MAD. Opening her clutch, she took out the full-length strap and secured it into place, dropping it over her shoulder. Bloody mad. She'd had the perfect opportunity to politely excuse herself and she'd hesitated.

She cursed herself as she watched him, his shirt sleeves rolled up. The muscles in his tanned forearm shifted as he signed the tab. His jacket hung over the nearby chair.

She had no problem saying no when she didn't want something. It was saying no when she did that was the problem.

As he walked towards her, she released an inner sigh; dammit, she was not in the habit of denying herself.

She smiled at the doorman as they left, and breathed in the dusky twilight, pulling London into her lungs. "I hope you left Jason a nice message?"

A lopsided grin lit his features. "Sure. I signed the tab and wrote, *'Jess says thanks'*."

She let the laugh lift through her, slowly nodding her head. "Nice."

As they headed onto Horse Guards Parade she became aware, with each footfall, how quiet the city had become. The sun had set but the pubs were yet to call time, and the parade was deserted.

The black and gold wrought iron gates of St. James's Park rose before them, and the scent of night stocks and lavender sat on the air, filling the easy silence between them. The sandstone path weaved its way towards the unseen Palace, and when his warm hand enclosed hers she didn't pull away.

He laced their fingers, his palm rough and solid as it met hers. She acknowledged the excited energy that pooled low in her belly. It'd been a long time. It was good to feel the spark of longing.

They seemed to drift down the neat path in haze of summer night air, the Tiffany Fountain slowly came into view as they rounded the bend, the cascading water reflecting myriad prisms of glittering lights as swans drifted across the lake. The soft skin of their wrists touched and his pulse beat too fast, as did hers. It was like a fairy tale.

Except something was wrong.

Her step faltered as unease moved through her. The warm, late summer evening was full of the flowery scents of August, but something prodded her conscious. She *felt* something watching them.

Opening her mind, she threw out a diaphanous web, tentatively searching for whatever had sent the sudden chill crawling up her spine.

Something was trailing her.

"You okay?"

His hushed voice calmed, as his firm grip steadied her.

"Yeah. Silly shoes is all." Looking up at him, she caught the serious edge to his voice, the tension filling his stance, and his gaze flicked all around them. Had he picked up on something too?

"Men are lucky." She looked pointedly at his brogued feet as they walked, drawing his attention down. "I mean, heels would look ridiculous with those trousers, but still, you know what I'm saying?"

His confused look told her she'd briefly distracted him, as she'd hoped, and she offered him a wide-eyed stare.

Shaking his head, he stared at her shoes. "I don't think I'd manage to walk in those. And you've got much better legs than me."

"Thanks." She gave him a sassy wink that left him chuckling, as she silently chanted the mirror spell. She hated—absolutely hated—to use mirror magic, but they were not completely alone in a dark park, and she was flash out of options. Now, all she needed was for him to close his eyes. "And I'm sure your legs are great."

His chuckle became a full-blown laugh, as he ran his hand through his hair, and she caught his mild embarrassment. The laughter lifted his tension, and heightened his energy, which would help her send this damn whatever-it-was running for the hills.

"Well, I'm not taking my trousers off here for you to find out." He gave her a knowing look filled with humor. "Men get arrested for doing that kind of thing in parks, you know."

Coming to a standstill, she planted both palms on her hips, and tapped her foot. She made him turn to face her, leaving his back to whatever was tagging along. "Afraid?"

Excitement tripped through her system as his heavy-lidded gaze clashed with hers and he stalked towards her, catching her around the waist.

Her breath caught in her throat as his chest pressed to hers. His shoulders were broad and solid beneath her palms, the soft silk of his shirt a direct contrast to the hardness of him.

He easily lifted her from the floor, allowing her to see the park behind him. And that was when she saw them: eyes, glinting from the undergrowth, watching them.

She cursed beneath her breath as she brought their lips together, furious that she wasn't able to just sink into him.

Her silent chanting beat a heavy drum within her as she pulled magic from deep down. Linking her arms around his neck, she faced her palms out, and making a final check that his eyes were shut, she released the spell.

The magic rushed through her system, bouncing from her palms in a silver electric rush. The circle of magic morphed into a ring of mirrors around them, coursing with the power of protection, a beam unerringly finding the creature in the trees.

The low groan sounded distinctly feminine, as whatever it was hissed, and smoke hazed the night air.

The power kept a thrumming rhythm within her, as his taste finally penetrated her senses. Letting her eyes drift shut, she breathed him in; his arms wrapped around her, the heat of him scorching through the sheer fabric of the back of her dress.

He tasted of whisky and the ocean. How was that even possible? She swept her tongue across his lips, teasing the soft skin of his bottom lip.

As his grasp eased, she slowly slid to the ground, releasing a soft moan as his hands settled at her waist, running a heated upward trail, his fingers touching her spine. A shiver swept her body as he traced the soft skin of her neck, to her hairline; his fingers ever so gently undoing her hair, dropping the pins to the ground.

Cupping her jaw, he took a final taste of her lips, before pulling back from her. Jess leant her head against his chest, catching her breath, calming herself and her magic, before lifting her gaze. High color flagged his cheekbones, and although his lips curved, he looked feral. She had the dangerous sensation of being hunted, and she liked it.

Sweeping her hair over one shoulder, she waited. What-

33

ever had been in the park had fled after taking a hit from her, but she wondered for how long.

"Jess?" The ever-darkening night hid him, and his rough voice was like a caress.

She bent down and picked up her clutch and his jacket, handing it to him. "Come on." She kept her voice low as she reached for his hand, pulling him away from the lake.

The brightly lit Mall lay beyond the gates, and the silence of the park faded away as cars and taxis streamed closer with each step.

As she walked through the gates, she caught her breath. It rarely happened these days, but the noise and light overwhelmed her, and just for a minute it was all too much, and she flinched at the energy overload.

Stepping in front of her, he seemed to be shielding her from the traffic, and she found herself reaching out to stroke the line of his back. The shirt was soft, but unable to conceal the strength of muscle beneath her fingertips.

Hailing a taxi, he opened the door, reaching for her hand to help her in to the black-cab.

He looked through the glass screen to the driver. "The Rembrandt." Before turning to her. "You okay?"

"Sure, it was just all a bit bright for a minute." She laughed self-consciously, and noticed the time. "The night's raced away..."

As the taxi pulled away, she felt her internal barriers kick back in, blocking out the constant hustle of London. She loved the thrum of life here, but if she let her guard slip it could also drain her dry.

He settled in beside her, and she felt him relax. "Hmm. I'm sure my excellent company had something to do with that."

She laughed, as she knew he'd hoped she would. "I think I'm pretty good company myself."

"Well, it beats sitting with the boring art buyer moaning about politics, doesn't it?"

She grinned and turned to him, surprised to find herself so close. The lights whizzed by, dancing

over his face. He had kind eyes, and it felt so natural to lean towards him, to brush her lips with

his. "More than beats it."

Easing back, she caught the surprise in his eyes. She'd overstepped. Somehow in the last handful of hours she'd crossed a line, with him and herself, she was lost somewhere between being flirty and feeling tender.

It was late, and she was high from magic and passion, and probably overloaded with outside energy as well as being empty of her own.

Looking away from him, out the window, she squeezed her eyes shut, and readied herself to make a flippant remark. But he touched her hand, coupling his with hers, and his softly mumbled 'good' silenced her.

The cab eased to a stop in front of his hotel, and she let go of his hand, watching his shirt pull taught across his shoulder blades as he opened the door and picked up his jacket. Her hand felt cold without his heat, and despite the excitement dancing through her, she knew she'd be monumentally stupid to get involved with someone from work. She'd only met him today—*and* he was a friend of Jason's.

The list of reasons against just kept getting longer.

Stepping from the cab he turned, holding his hand towards her.

"Come with me?" His expression gave nothing away, but his eyes...they told a completely different story.

Opening her mouth to say no, it crept up on her; the malice, untempered hunger, that feeling of being watched, preyed upon.

It was back.

Offering him a smile, she tilted her head, playing for time while she honed in on the source. "That probably wouldn't be smart."

It was off to her left, close to the hotel. Glancing over her shoulder, she could almost pick-up something in the shadow between the buildings. Dammit, she could leave him and go after it, but it could also double back and take a shot a Seb. It would be safer to stay with him. *Yeah, whatever you need to tell yourself.* She cursed her little voice.

"Probably not." His voice was hushed. "Come with me anyway."

His hand was sure and steady as he waited for her.

Jess could feel the palpable disappointment of whatever was stalking her, when she placed her hand in his. Not sure what to make of that, or how she was going to handle Seb, she let him pull her from the cab.

She lightly held his wrist as he went to press the button for the elevator, halting him. "I'm going to come up, but there can't be any funny business."

His head tipped as he looked at her—studied her. She searched for any sign of what he might be thinking, surprised when the grin lit his face.

Gently pulling from her grip he pressed the button, the elevator doors opening before them. "'Funny business'. I like that."

The air thickened as the doors closed, and Jess firmed her lips, realizing she'd just made herself sound like an uptight spinster. Catching his gaze, he was still smirking, and she crunched her nose at him, flicking her hair as she lifted her chin. "You know what I mean; we work together, you're a friend of Jason's, *I'm* a friend of Jason's—it would get awkward..."

≈

SEB LEANT back against the wall, sliding his hands in pockets. "Why? Are you and Jason involved?" He knew full well they weren't, but he was curious to see her reaction.

Her eyes widened as she turned to fully face him, her jaw virtually hanging open. "No! Gross, that's just—there are no words. None. Gross." She sliced her hand in front of her, as if to enunciate her statement. He hid his smug look behind a laugh.

"Well, okay then." He waited a heartbeat before adding, "So what's the problem?"

She slitted her eyes at him, playful annoyance sparkling in their depths. "You *know* what the problem is." She poked him none too lightly in the back, as she followed him down the plushly carpeted corridor to his room. "We're going to be in offices across the hall from each other, and when this ends we're still going to have to work together."

Holding the door ajar so she could walk past him into the room, he dropped the key card and his jacket on the dressing table. "So negative, Jessica." He raised his brow, deliberately baiting her. "Who says it has to end?"

She closed her mouth with a snap, both her brows arched. "Oh, bugger off. Other young things might fall for that, but I'm totally not having this discussion. Besides—"

He cut her off from whatever else she'd been about to say. "Good. We'll cross that bridge when we come to it, then. Drink?" He left her stood near the balcony doors, and walked off smiling to himself. He liked her, liked her sharp temper and quick mouth.

Staring into the well-stocked minibar in the private kitchenette, he closed his eyes at the thought of her mouth. He definitely liked that.

The glasses weren't the heavy crystal they'd been drinking out of, and the scotch wasn't as good. But then, you couldn't have everything. He added a bowl of ice to the tray, and headed back to the main room.

Her clutch was lying on his jacket, her shoes left by the closed balcony doors, and she was outside, leaning on the railing looking down onto the street.

Opening the door, he looked questioningly at her as she whipped round with a smile.

"Okay?" Looking round her at the quietening city, he raised his shoulders. "Much to look at out here?"

"Nope, nothing. It's chilling down too. Inside is better."

She slid past him, as he stared to the street below. A caustic smoke tinged the air, irritating his eyes. Pulling the door closed, he drew the heavy drapes. "Smells like burning rubber out there."

"Hmmm." She briefly agreed as she touched the screen on the neat Bluetooth system, scrolling through the hotel's music before finally settling on something bluesy. "This place is so nice, you won't want to leave."

Coming towards her, he slid his arm around her dainty waist, before taking her hand and placing it on his chest, gently easing her to him to softly sway with the music.

The top of her head barely brushed his chin without her shoes on. Her breasts cushioned against his chest, the petal soft skin of her hand in his left his heart pounding a heavy rhythm, as lust sank through his system. Which he reckoned she couldn't fail to notice, as the heavy weight of his shaft pressed against her hip.

He looked down, to find a warm smile on her beautiful face. "What?"

"So. We're dancing then?" Her voice had a husky quality, as if she'd just woken from sleep. She lightly adjusted his collar as she spoke.

As she angled her head back to look up him, her dark hair brushed his arm as he held her, the silky locks sent shivers across the skin. The dip of her spine through the sheer fabric of her dress sent heat rising up his back.

She fit perfectly to him, every lush curve, and he didn't question the urge to taste her sweet lips. Cupping the back of her head, easing his fingers through the fall of her hair, he breathed her in, took her mouth.

Sweeping his tongue against her own, he came to a standstill as their heavy breaths filled his ears. She'd gone up on her toes, sliding her arms around his shoulders, pulling him down to her. Her hungry kiss egged him on.

Bending down, he deftly lifted her into his arms, not breaking their kiss.

Lifting her closer allowed him better access to her sweetness, and he nipped at her lips, as he headed for the couch.

Backing down into the dark leather, he settled in, adjusting her on his lap.

Her long legs lay across the cushions, and he couldn't help reaching out, smoothing his palm up the sleek length of her calf, curving his hand around the back of her knee and sweeping up her thigh.

As he slid beneath the hem of her dress, he groaned at the feel of the stocking top. The satiny band gave way to even silkier flesh, and his heart just about beat out of his chest at the thought of what she wore under the confines of her clothes.

His fingers reached the edge of something lacy that curved high across her buttock and he gripped the sweet weight, loving how the rich curve gave beneath his molding grasp.

She gasped lightly against his lips, the sound lost in his heated kiss, as she splayed her hands across his shoulders pulling away, resting her forehead against his chest.

"Seb..." Her voice trailed off as she caught her breath.

He waited her out, tracing circles across the exposed skin

at the back of her thigh. The dress had ridden up, pulled taught across his forearm, revealing the neatly banded hold-ups. He wanted to lick the skin visible there, with hot, wet, open-mouthed kisses, and discover what a luscious piece she was.

Until she finally lifted her head, her lips heavy and full from his. "Seb," she broke off, and shook her head, a lilt of laughter in her voice as she spoke. "I have no idea what to say." Curling her legs towards her, he sadly had no choice but to remove his hand from the lush warmth of her skin.

She angled herself more fully in his lap, the weight of her soft ass not helping the raging pressure in his cock, as he braced his legs further apart, letting her fall between them.

"But I won't stay." Her gaze was full of disappointment as she said the words, and she ruefully looked at him. "You. You are a surprise."

Sliding his hands round her waist, he linked his fingers at her back, enjoying having her pressed more fully to him. "I could probably convince you to stay." He let his grin be deliberately lascivious, and pulled her more firmly against the heavy weight of him.

She chuckled, even as her neat, white teeth worried her bottom lip. "Yeah, you probably could. But why don't we just work together for a bit and see?"

He nodded slowly, curious as to how long they could hold off the attraction that burned between them. "Okay, if that's what you want."

His embrace tightened as she went to rise. "Where you going?"

She looked questionably at him. "Well, home. I'll see you at work tomorrow."

"You don't have to rush off just because we're not gonna..." he waggled his eyebrows at her, "...you know."

Her laughter was soft as she relaxed, laying her head on

his chest. "Even though we're not...ya know... It's late—or more likely bloody early. I should still go."

~

A GOOD SOLID metaphysical shove from her brother brought Jess instantly awake. Her breath lodged in her throat as she blinked, trying to clear her vision.

The heavy rise and fall of Seb's chest beneath her cheek had her scrunching her eyes tightly back shut.

What had she done? A mental assessment told her they both still had their clothes on, and as she came fully to her senses, she loosely remembered dropping off to sleep as they'd lay on the couch talking.

Opening her eyes, she stared down the length of their bodies, her legs entwined with his. The lamp within his reach had been switched off, only the warm glow from the hall tipped into the room. His arm tightened around her as she shifted, his breathing deepened beneath her palm, as he stroked her hip.

Nothing would please her more than to lay her head back down, but as she felt another remote nudge from Adam she knew something must be wrong.

Her knees touched the plush carpet as she carefully rolled off the couch, easing out from under his arm. Grabbing her shoes, she turned for her clutch, briefly stopping to look down at him.

The top few buttons of Seb's shirt were undone, revealing a tanned collar bone. He'd thrown one arm above his head, and all the tension had melted from his peaceful features. His nose was straight and proud, the same as his jaw. His lips had softly parted, his hair falling back from his forehead. She smiled. He reminded her of a sleeping prince, and she'd have liked nothing better than to wake him with a kiss.

41

But it wasn't to be. Catching the time on the tiny alarm clock next to the bed, she rolled her eyes; 4.44 am. She was going to be tired. Grabbing her clutch, she looked at the hotel pad and paper next to the phone. Should she leave him a note? What would she say anyway?

She'd be at work with him in a few hours.

She'd buy him a coffee on her way in. Clicking the door shut, she stood in the deserted corridor, and held her breath, before laying her palm flat against wood.

She racked her brain for a spell that wouldn't mark him, but that would still protect him, wishing that just for once she had her sister's dedication to study and spell craft.

Everything she thought of would leave a mystical signature on him, and she just couldn't risk that.

Dropped her palm she rushed away; she'd whipped out onto Seb's balcony last night, the minute he'd gone to get drinks, and found the wild-eyed creature hovering in the shadow barely a few feet away, the shiny blonde crop of hair catching the streetlights.

It had been trying to see in. Jess had been so stunned that she'd just reacted, and had sent it ricocheting between the buildings down to the alley below.

Her common sense told her that it wouldn't come back looking for more, but worry and doubt niggled at her as she left the hotel, rushing round the corner to her place.

As she turned the key in the lock, the sound of her mobile echoed through the flat. "Well, what do you know, the phone lives after all."

Running to grab it from the coffee table, she wasn't surprised to see the caller ID as Adam.

"Brother dear, what the hell... Is everything alright?" She dropped to the sofa.

"Bloody hell, Jess, why don't you answer your phone!"

He all but roared at her, and tangled up with his annoyance she detected pain and worry.

Pushing up, she gripped the phone tightly, as the line crackled and hissed. "Adam, what's the matter?" Her voice still as she waited.

"I'm okay." His voice instantly dropped, calming, as he detected the panic in hers. "I'm pissed off, but I'm okay—I've broken my leg. I'm in a Greek hospital and I don't speak enough Greek, and they want to operate and..." His voice trailed away and her eyes widened at the small whispers of fear she heard in his voice.

"Adam, hey now." Her tone softened. She hated not being able to get straight to him. "I can come. Do you want me to come?"

Normally he'd brush her off, tell her he was fine. But not today. The pause before he spoke was enough for her.

"I don't want to be out of it, and here alone." The finality in his tone fired her into action.

"Okay, where are you? I'll phone Thea and we'll fly ou—"

His sharp 'No' stopped her.

"Not Thea, don't tell her yet. Promise me, Jess."

She slumped back, unable to process it, they never lied to each other. "Adam, I don't... We can't keep things from Thea—"

"Jess please, this place is heaving. There must be dozens of people in the corridors alone. I just want you to come in and get me out. I don't want Thea to have to deal with all these people, she's been so much better." His voice trailed away, and Jess thought of their sister, and how much she'd suffered when the magic had first come upon them, and how deeply she was affected by the over-powering emotions of others. Adam was right... sort of.

"Okay, but you have to tell her. Today. Before she knows something's wrong—and she will know. I'll phone her later, and fudge it somehow; tell her I'm coming to get you, or something." Her mind darted with possibilities of what to tell their sister, gods she'd be angry if she found out.

She scribbled notes as he told her where he was, rapidly running through what to do next.

Pulling off her dress as she raced around, dialing the airline, she left it on loudspeaker as she rummaged through her luggage and handbag, pulling out her passport and anything she thought to throw into a small backpack.

Managing to book a flight into Athens, she nearly cried at the thought of the little island hopper she'd have to charter to fly up country to Myrina. Little planes shook and wobbled. Her stomach roiled at the thought. Dammit, she hated planes.

Slamming out of the flat, she dialed for a cab, and waited until she was safely seated inside before trying to call Jason.

By the third try she was about ready to hex him when he finally answered.

"Jason! Thank the gods. Adam's been in an accident, I've got to fly out to get him."

"Jess! Slow down. Where are you?"

She took a breath, holding it for a second to still her racing heart.

"Still in London. Adam's broken his leg, in Greece. He *asked* for help."

Jason's softly muttered 'It must be bad' made her laugh around the sudden lump in her throat.

"That's what I thought." The whispered words scratched as tears stung her vision. "I know I'm working this week, but—"

"Jesus, Jess, this is your family. Are you boarding?"

"No, just coming out of London now."

"Right then—get out there and let me know when everything's alright, okay?" He slightly paused before adding, "Did you enjoy last night's gala?" The thread of humor in his voice was designed to distract, and she closed her eyes, leaning back, thankful for the best friend she could've asked for.

Her laugh sounded watery even to her own ears. "You sod. Leaving us to sit with that motley crew."

His snicker was a balm to her wired nerves.

"I try. Keep in touch, Sweetheart."

She sighed and shut her eyes as the cab trailed through the early morning rush-hour, heading for the airport.

CHAPTER 4

JESS ARCHED HER BACK. Three weeks of traveling, hotels and hospitals had taken its toll. The thick coating of packed waiting rooms, departure lounges, and vending machine coffee had seeped into her skin. Exhaustion had settled deep, and she couldn't remember what silence felt like.

Adam sat next to her in the cab, his blue eyes closed, his amber lashes splayed against the dark circles that had taken up permanent residence. The cast encasing his left leg was awkwardly perched on the seat in front of him.

Two surgeries and a wonderful doctor had kept them in Greece until he was convinced that Adam was safe to fly. Never had she been so pleased to be on a plane circling the Thames.

But the cab they were in was leaving London behind, heading out of the city, ever southbound.

Pulling her phone from her pocket, she stifled a yawn as she texted Jason, letting him know they'd landed and were heading home. She closed her eyes for what felt like seconds when the phone vibrated in her palm.

Get some rest, and that's an order ;)

Take your couple of weeks' holiday. I'm bound to have work that you can do there and you can stay on a bit longer.

We've got everything under control here.

Jase x

Seb's smiling face raced across her mind, she wanted to ask Jason to let him know that everything was okay, she'd wanted to talk to him countless times over the last weeks, but it sounded daft to her over-tired, over-worried brain. She'd just have to wait and see what happened when she went back to work.

Staring out of the window, she let her mind drift. The motorway was far behind, and the orange streetlights streamed down, glaring into the windows, making her flinch with each pass. If her energy was at an all-time low, she had no idea how Adam was still functioning; his ward had been packed with people, the constant coming and going of nurses and gurneys, all through the night.

Scrunching her tired eyes at the thought, she rolled down the window as quietly as could, not wanting to disturb what little rest he could get.

The London cab rolled across the single lane bridge onto the Island, doubtlessly looking out of place against the rural backdrop. The few remaining posts of the old train bridge rose from the sea, running parallel to them as they drove, barely visible against the night sky.

Jess stared out of the back window. Langstone Bay lay behind them. The lights from the pub reflected onto the water, the little village where their sister lived was all battened down. The pub would have only a few regulars sitting at the bar on this quiet Wednesday night.

A ghost of a smile touched her lips, as she watched the pretty pub fade into the misty night. Give Adam a few days to rest up, and maybe they could have dinner there. Just the three of them.

The yearning for her family hit her so quickly she caught her breath, and rapidly blinked away silly, weary tears.

Turning her face into the September breeze, she breathed in the peace, and the salt and pine tinged air. The gentle tide polished the pebbles as it crept up the beach and the road weaved through the darkness, traveling deeper onto the Island.

As they left the sea behind, horse fields surrounded them, leading to little roads with bungalows. They passed the stables where they'd all learnt to ride as kids, the farm shop that would soon be full of pumpkins.

The past bled into her, and the silence she'd been longing for slowly started to seep into her soul.

The taxi pulled into a quiet road lined with a handful of cottages and cherry trees.

Jess sat up straighter, loving the gentle feeling that swept through her at the sight of her home. The white walls and low slate roof were softly illuminated by her outside lights, and Thea stood in the shadow of the open front door, her soft blonde curls haloed in the porch light.

More stupid tears filled her vision as she leant over, grabbing Adam's hand. "Hey. You awake? We're home."

His bright blue gaze mirrored the joy in hers, as he struggled to sit up and caught sight of Thea.

Easing her aching body from the cab, Jess leant down so that Adam could brace himself on her shoulder, as he balanced on one leg, placing his plastered foot softly to the ground, all the while cursing the crutches.

She'd barely got him standing up when Thea was on them.

She was inches shorter than the pair of them, but that didn't stop her wrapping them up, her own unique scent of jasmine swirling around them.

Her soft laughter was watery with emotion as she hugged them.

Adam's voice sounded gruff as he spoke, his grip tight around the pair of them. "Gods, it's good to be here."

Sniffing, laughing and dashing at more tears, Jess maneuvered him indoors, as Thea hurried back and forth pulling in their luggage.

Awkwardly stumbling, Jess finally got him to the couch, and with an unceremonious twist she let his weight bring him to the sofa, before rolling her eyes at him. "Dude, you're going to have to get better at this." Humor lit her gaze as he politely told her to sod off, until the low whine brought her attention whipping round.

Murphy sat perfectly still in front of the patio doors, his black ears hanging low with worry.

Jess stepped back as she watched him come to his paws and pad across the hardwood floor, before slowly getting onto the sofa where he sat down, next to Adam, his solemn Labrador eyes studying his owner, searching for himself that everything was okay.

The lump swelled in Jess's throat as Thea came to stand beside her, reaching for her hand, watching the exchange.

"Hey there, Murph." Adam's voice was hardly a whisper as he reached up to stroke Murphy's face.

"You don't need to look at me like that, fella, it's just a broken leg."

Murphy slowly eased his front paws across Adam's thighs. Laying his head down in his lap, he gave a huff and closed his eyes. He had clearly decided Adam needed guarding.

"He's been okay all summer. We've had great fun while you were off gallivanting, but once he knew you were hurt..." Thea's equally soft voice trailed away.

Jess smiled as she bent, smoothing his ears and gently

readjusting his collar, working her voice past the lump in her throat. "That's because he's a very, very good boy."

The over-emotional state of the pair of them fired Thea into action, and Jess found herself route-marched off to bed, with instructions to get a good night's rest.

The gentle sun warmed the side of her face, slowly tugging her from sleep. Opening her eyes, Jess lay still, her own white sheets and duvet wrapped around her. The sun beamed in through the lace net curtains, making shadowy shapes on the soft white ceiling.

She'd hadn't bothered with the full curtains last night, she'd barely got her clothes off before collapsing into bed, safe in the knowledge that Thea was handling everything.

The ornate mantel clock next to her bed said it was after six. Jess stretched, before kneeling up to look out of the window above her bed. Moving the net out of the way she opened the window, staring out. Her little garden had no back fence, only a short white wall with a gate, that lead straight to the beach. The yellow grass and peaks of the sand dunes drawing the eye to the calm ocean, and further, all the way to the horizon.

Pulling in huge lungfuls of clean air, she pushed her hair back from her face. She felt amazing, like she'd slept for a week. Arching her back, she found no aches and pains left over from hours sat in waiting rooms; no tension left across her neck from worry and waiting.

Shaking her head, she came to a stop as she padded round her room. At the foot of her bed was a pretty selenite spiral, softly glowing with the hue of magic.

Carefully picking it up, she felt her sister's energy radiating from the crystal as she turned it towards the light; Thea's magic had clearly become much stronger, she could feel it pulsing against her palms. The mending and rejuvenating spell was a bolt of pure healing energy to her senses.

Placing it on her bedside table, she gathered Adam would have one too, so he should wake feeling a hell of a lot better than yesterday.

Keeping her fingers crossed that a good night's sleep would help his mood, she pulled on her white kimono dressing-gown, smiling as she headed out into her home. The early autumn sun streamed in through the windows, bathing the hardwood floors and surfaces. The warmth beneath the soles of her feet lifted her spirits even more, as did Murphy's welcoming bark as he came to greet her, nudging her thigh.

"Hey there, did you sleep okay?" Kneeling down, she took his face in her hands, nuzzling his velvety head.

Pulling back, she waited as he looked at her, checking her over before giving her a toothy grin.

"You've clearly had a good night's rest too, Murph." As she stroked down his head she found a small piece of selenite, encased in a spiral holder, hanging from his collar. The worry had disappeared from his aura, and Jess breathed a sigh of relief; her equilibrium was settling back down. Thea had been very busy indeed.

Entering the kitchen, she found her brother and her sister sitting at her little table, his leg propped up on a chair.

"And I thought I was up early." Knowing it would annoy him, Jess ruffled Adam's auburn hair as she walked by, getting just past the reach of his crutch as he went to jab her with it. "Now-now, I came all the way to get you. Be nice."

Grinning at him, she squeezed Thea's shoulder as went, before flopping down into a chair and reaching for the teapot. Gesturing between them with her cup, she raised her brows at her brother. "Oh, and I had a fabulous night's sleep. How about you, Adam?"

He turned curious blue eyes to Thea, and nodded, as Thea squirmed in her chair. "Funny that, me too. Must have been some pretty powerful mojo. What did you do, Thea?"

Jess kept her eye on Thea as she poured her tea. It had been a year or so since she'd last been home, and Thea had been knee-deep wrapping up her PhD.

When the magic had come into them, Thea had been hit the hardest. She'd been home for the summer, getting ready to head back to uni for the autumn term when it happened— maybe the constant overload of energy, from the masses of people in London, had been too much for a new witch to handle. Jess didn't know. But Thea had barely been able to finish her degree, before coming back to the bay.

Jess and Adam had watched her struggle just to leave the house at first. It had taken months. But as Jess studied her sister, it was clear all that had changed.

"Just gave you both a little boost, that's all. The selenite is a great conduit for that." Her wide brown eyes glanced between them over her cup, and Jess slitted her vision at all she wasn't saying.

Placing both elbows on the table, Jess pinned her sister with a look. "Okay. Spill it."

Adam nodded in agreement, leaning into a more comfortable position.

Letting out a puff, Thea blew her curly bangs from her eyes, shrugging off their curiosity. "Truthfully? I'm still working it all out. I've been trying to find a way to create a barrier for myself, so that the energy of others doesn't drain me as much. And the process of doing that has meant I've put in some hard study hours." She placed her cup down, neatly folding her palms in front of her.

Jess waited, until it become obvious that she wasn't going to add anything else. "And?"

"The side effect of which has been my spell crafting has got good, and that's made my magic stronger... Quite a bit stronger."

Jess watched Adam tap his finger against the side of his

cup. She felt his curiosity rising when he said, "But have you managed to barrier others' emotions?"

"Yes." Thea held up her hands, as they both leant forward, ready to pepper her with questions. "I mean, I couldn't move back to the City or anything—I wouldn't want to anyway now. But yes, I have found, as the magic has grown it's helped me too. I was unconsciously holding it at bay, and the more I've opened up and let it in, the more it's protected me." She waited a beat before adding, "And heightened my senses." Clearing her throat, Thea's brows furrowed as she frowned at them, and Jess waited, knowing a telling-off was coming their way, just not sure why.

"For instance, don't keep things from me. I bloody know the pair of you concocted some story to supposedly 'protect' me while all this has been going on, and I won't bloody have it."

Looking guiltily at Adam, Jess gave him a mental poke as she frowned at him. *I told you!* Before turning to Thea, her apology dying in her throat as she watched an emerald green swirl through her sister's brown eyes.

"Thea! Your eyes!"

Waving her hand she shushed her, and Jess snapped her mouth shut, sitting back in her chair.

"Don't go changing the subject, Jess. I'm bloody cross."

Adam cleared his throat, struggling to hide his grin, and Jess hurriedly looked down into her lap, smothering her own smirk. They'd never been able to take Thea's temper seriously; she'd always been the one to wade in and stop their battles, she'd always been their anchor.

Taking a big sip of his coffee, amusement laced his gaze as he looked over at Thea, and Jess was surprised to see the absolute relief in his eyes.

"I'm sorry. I asked Jess not to worry you." He put down his cup and grasped Thea's hand across the table. "But Sweetheart, I'm so pleased for you. If your eyes are finally changing, you really must be getting stronger..." His voice trailed away as he waited for Thea to explain, and Jess wondered, not for the first time, how much more Adam knew about their magic that he wasn't sharing.

Turning a warm smile on her brother, Thea laughed. "I am stronger, and I have been for a long time, but we just haven't all been together in so long, that I haven't been able to tell you."

The flood of guilt hit Jess's system, but she'd didn't get to voice her thoughts before Thea turned on her.

"And don't do that—no guilt. Our lives are busy and hectic and all over the place. I should've just told you, but I was keeping it like a secret—a wonderful secret that I wanted to share with you

both, when we were all together."

Jess sighed, holding Thea's free hand, and taking Adam's in her other hand, she linked them.

The bolt of magic raced between them, making her laugh at the force of it. "No guilt. And no secrets. You're right, I'm sorry." Giving Thea a wink, she squeezed her hand. "How often are your eyes changing?"

Breaking the circle, Thea rubbed her temple as she rolled her eyes heavenward, the brown and green depths still swirling together.

"Ugh, it's all the time! I tell you, a little bit of emotion and...boom. It's bloody hard to explain away too."

Jess laughed with delight as Adam frowned. So there really was a man on the scene! She'd thought so when they'd last spoken, but they'd all had this broken-Adam business to deal with, and she hadn't had time to go digging for the story.

Jess barely held the giggle in, sitting on her hands to stop herself from rubbing her palms together. She couldn't wait to see Adam deal with this one.

Getting up from the table, she rummaged through the cupboards, looking for food. Coming out with a loaf of bread and some waffles, she looked at Thea. "Try contact lenses."

"Well, that's what I said to Marc... That's what I said when it happened, but it's a bit lame, Jess."

Watching Adam's head snap up as Thea stammered over the mention of a man, Jess kept her laughter buried deep. Good for Thea.

"No, you loon. Not as an excuse. Actually get some brown contacts, that's what I do."

Thea's laughter bubbled up as she came to help in the kitchen, "Oh. Of course! I get you."

Catching her brother now frowning heavily at both of them, she offered him a little grin. He couldn't protect them from everything.

CHAPTER 5

THREE WEEKS LATER

JESS STARED out of the window and wished she was sat on the pebble beach. She'd wrap her arms around her bent legs as the tide lapped the shore and the sun beat down.

But it wasn't going to happen.

The supposed *amazing* summer that she'd hardly seen a glimpse of had passed-by while she wasn't looking, and now the sad, grey rain tapped against the glass and dripped down to the old wooden frame, blurring the beach outside.

Adam's need to stay with her had ended, and he'd taken his bad mood and moved back to his own house: a house that, unlike her bungalow, had stairs leading to the first floor and down to the sea. She let a little-sister smirk cross her face; she could picture him cursing that cast, as he thumped about his house.

Resting her forehead against the cold window, she thought about the nineteen hours in airports and on planes it had taken to reach him in Greece, and a week of rowing with him that he couldn't fly for seven days after such major surgery, before she'd even been able to attempt the nightmare that getting him home had been.

In the last couple of weeks, she'd put up with his huffing and puffing, his frustration and constant anger at being forced to take it easy, until finally she thought she'd strangle him if he didn't give her some peace.

But now he'd gone. Thea had driven him and Murphy back to his, and she was left rattling around here.

The stillness was complete, the sea barely whispered above the rain, and autumn was getting ready to hand over to winter.

Murphy's four paws weren't padding across her living room carpet, he wasn't flopping down in front of the warm fire, dreaming about chasing squirrels.

It was too quiet.

As the early evening darkness crept in, the lamp behind her cast her own reflection in the glass. Her sullen face looked sulky, and she frowned at herself before turning away.

She could go out, take a drive, maybe stop somewhere. She slid her hands into her warm soft pockets and looked down. Thick pink socks and dark-green jogging pants looked back up at her. She grinned at her feet and shrugged.

"Well, I'm not getting changed again." So she clearly wasn't going anywhere.

She peered down the hallway as the headlights reflected through her front porch window, and a car pulled onto her drive.

Opening the front door, Jess leant against the door-jamb as Thea parked the rumbling Land Rover. Despite the well-cared-for engine, the bodywork had definitely seen better days.

Jess grinned as her sister clambered out, with her long-legged Labrador pup close at her heels as they made a mad dash for the house.

Poppy skidded into the hallway, tail wagging furiously as she grinned up at Jess, her bright brown eyes full of mischief and laughter.

"Well, aren't you happy with yourself, young lady." Jess used both hands to smooth her silky, soft ears, rubbing her cheek against Poppy's.

The young pup's bubbly energy filtered through her palms. The innocent joy warmed her heart, and Jess made sure to give her a wink and a smile.

Thea shut the door on the wind and rain, and leant back against it, blowing upwards against her curly blonde bangs that hung in her eyes.

"It's filthy out there!" With a laugh, she hugged Jess tight.

Jess took a moment to let her sister's beautiful calmness sink into her, even if she was dripping wet.

"And what brings you out on this disgusting night?" Jess held the cuff of Thea's enormous raincoat, pulling as Thea attempted to extract herself from its folds. Poppy pranced around their feet, thoroughly enjoying this new game.

"Marc is up to his eyes trying to get his patient files together so we can go up to York for a couple of weeks. I thought I'd give him some peace, and as you've been broadcasting your misery so loudly for the last couple of hours, I figured you could use some company."

Jess rolled her eyes and headed to the kitchen, muttering under her breath, "I haven't been that bad."

"Oh please, you've been sending out moany vibes all evening."

Giving her sister an 'oh really' look, Jess filled the kettle and placed it on the gas, busying herself getting cups from the cupboard.

She turned to find Thea leaning against the sink, with Poppy calmly sitting at her heels.

Within days of being back in the bay, it hadn't taken Jess

long to discover that Thea was in the depths of heartbreak. She thanked the goddess daily that Adam had been incapacitated for long enough that Thea and Marc had managed to work it all out, before he could wade in like a bull in a china shop.

Now she was all loved up, and they were living in and out of each other's houses, raising the beautiful Poppy between them.

She expected engagement announcements any day now, and she couldn't wait for a hectic, noisy wedding.

"Have I really been broadcasting that badly?" Jess let out a sigh, shaking her dark hair back from her face. "I don't miss him or anything." The words sounded defensive even to her, and Thea's little chuckle didn't make her feel any better.

"Of course you don't. That's why you're moping about this place in god-awful sweat pants at six o'clock in the evening."

"I *like* these sweat pants."

Jess spooned jasmine tea leaves into the pot, and breathed in the aroma as she poured boiling water over them. "It's crazy, Thea. Come yesterday morning I was ready to kill him. And I'm not even kidding. But this place is so quiet without him and Murph."

She stirred the pot and left it to steep before turning to face her sister. "And I like my own company, dammit." She dropped the spoon on the side with a clatter, continuing to frown at Thea. "And don't you stand there smiling."

Jess let Thea usher her into a chair at the kitchen table, before her sister went back to carry over the tea things.

"I've been smiling since the two of you came home. You know how much I love having you both here."

Jess felt a slight lift in her dark mood, and offered Thea a self-deprecating smile. "I know—so have I. I'm being an idiot. I've enjoyed having Adam under my feet, even enjoyed him being a royal pain in the ass." Leaning round Thea, she offered Poppy a smile and held out a biscuit.

With a lot more enthusiasm than manners, her tail propelled her to Jess for the treat, before thumping rhythmically against the hardwood floor as she sat. "And it's Murphy I miss more than Adam, isn't that right, Poppy, hmmm?"

Jess figured Poppy would agree with just about anything she said for another biscuit, and with a laugh she rubbed her yellow chin. "Good girl."

Picking up her cup, she wrapped her hands around the warm china, glad Thea had turned up to save her from her pity-party-for-one.

"I'm totally with you. I missed Murph something awful. He was with me the whole summer; my place was so empty without him. But now look! I have this mischievous Miss to contend with."

Poppy looked between the two of them, soaking up being the center of attention.

"How do you think Adam will manage being back at his place?"

Jess rolled her eyes. "Who knows? He's still in the cast, he's got stairs to cope with, and Murphy glued to his side, checking that he's *okay* every minute of the day." She air quoted the okay, and grinned a little at that thought. "But at least he only has himself to moan to." Placing her cup down, she looked up at Thea. "Did you speak to him about Sarah?"

The energy in the warm kitchen thickened around them, and Jess knew with certainty that at the mention of her name their ancestor was making her presence known.

Thea's brown eyes locked with Jess's, as they both acknowledged they were no longer alone.

"I tried. I said that she'd come to me, to apologize. I was starting to explain that she had offered us the choice of being able to *give* our magic back. But I didn't get that far. He cut me off, saying 'the past is done, we can't change it.' Then he stomped off before I could get into his thick skull, that's precisely what he could do, if he wanted to."

Jess shook her head, going back to frowning—seemingly her default expression on this wet, wintery evening. "I don't understand him. If magic makes him so angry, then he needs to talk about it. To us. Magic is a part of who we are, and I certainly don't want to give mine back. Doesn't he want to know where we came from? I mean, you wouldn't have Marc if things had been different."

Thea set her cup down, her expression very solemn. "And I nearly didn't. When I finally understood that my best friend *and* my partner were both tied to me because of Sarah's actions I thought I'd lose them. I thought I'd have to... I don't know... let them go or give them up or something. There's still so much left to understand about how our two families are tied together."

Jess stared into her cup as she sipped, still certain that Adam knew more than he was letting on.

As she got to the bottom, the shadowy leaves churned in the last few remaining sips, and as she'd always done, she passed the cup to Thea.

Wrapping both hands around the cup, Thea turned it three times, before setting it down on the table, peering inside.

It always irked Jess that she'd never been able to read the cards or the leaves, but it wasn't her skill to master. Thea's gift was in reading the future, and Jess's in reading the past.

She watched as Thea formed a circle above the cup, and pooled magic in her palms; the silvery-green sparks formed around her hands and the leaves rose, flitting like birds inside the bubble she had created.

As children, their grandmother had taught them to read leaves, the old fashioned way—by tipping them into the saucer. Jess smiled as she imagined how happy Nanna would be now, to see them use the magic she'd always believed they carried.

As Thea waited for the images to become clear, the energy around them thrummed with power, as the spirits took their place in the ether.

"The river is calling you back." Thea's voice became hushed as she offered what the spirits revealed. "The crown symbolizes a royal request. The balance scales sway wildly, everything is out of kilter. You must make a choice as to where your loyalties lie."

Thea released her breath, and little taps against the window let them know the spirits had left.

Coming to her feet, Jess took a tin of mint humbugs from the cupboard, and placing six in a smooth crystal bowl, she put it on the window ledge, whispering her thanks.

"Well, clearly the leaves think you're going on some new journey. Where are you off to?"

Sitting back down, Jess idly stroked Poppy's soft head as she laid it in her lap offering comfort, thinking of all the leaves had revealed.

"We've got a new exhibition due to open at the Museum —that could represent the royal request. The last of the artifacts has been arriving this week, and I know Jason is eager to start getting it all sorted. He'd brought another historian on board just before I left, so at least he's had help."

Jess carefully cleared her mind as she talked about Seb, not wanting Thea to ask questions. It's not like she knew the answers anyway. A few hours asleep in his arms, and she couldn't stop thinking about him.

"I've done as much of the legwork from here as I can, and as much as I enjoy being here with you two fools, I'll have to get back before the end of the week." She raised a brow at

Thea, shrugging off the nerves at the thought of seeing Seb. "When are you off to York?"

Catching the knowing look Thea leveled at her, Jess knew that she'd only briefly been let off the hook.

"I've got two weeks off when term breaks, and I think we're aiming to spend as much of that in York as possible. So I've got a couple of days to get sorted, by which time Adam's leg should be in a lighter cast. Which means it should be okay to leave him." Thea waited a beat before raising her brows at Jess with a grin. "Right?"

Jess laughed at how ridiculous they were being. "He's a grown man! Why are we running around after him?"

Thea pushed up from the table and put her own cup in the sink and Jess's on the window ledge. "Beats me." She gestured at the cup. "Don't forget to return those leaves to the Earth."

She called Poppy to follow as she headed out of the kitchen.

Jess opened the front door and stared out at the rain, as Poppy sat down next to her while Thea wrestled with her coat.

Hugging her sister tight, Thea looked up at her. "I bet you can't wait to get back to London. The bay is still a bit too quiet for you."

There was no question in her words, and Jess just nodded.

As Thea and Poppy drove away, she looked up at the heavy clouds, breathing deeply. Salt tinged the air, as did the scent of the falling leaves. The street was silent, and the orange street lights glared down at the pavement.

London was never silent. Neither was Rome or Sydney, or any number of the other beautiful places she'd been lucky enough to go to.

But she'd loved the peace she'd found here in these last weeks.

Turning back into the warm, she shut the door, mentally packing her case. She was heading off to Cologne at the weekend, not London, she was booked to evaluate a religious relic next week. Why had the leaves seen the river?

Picking her phone up from the kitchen side, the incoming message buzzed in her hand.

The V&A needs you more than Cologne.
Can you be in LDN by Friday?
Skype me and I'll explain.
Jason

That answered that question, then. The light chuckle on the air had her poking her tongue out to a last remaining spirit. "That's a quick answer, even for you guys." She felt the laughter surround her before hearing a final tap against the window, leaving her completely alone, and glancing at the empty crystal bowl on the window ledge, she realized she'd been fleeced of mint humbugs too.

Texting him back, she pressed 'send' before dropping the phone on the coffee table and turning to the fire. She placed some logs on the dwindling embers, and gave it a zap with her right hand, sending the fire snapping to life. Everything accomplished, she headed to the fridge for a glass of wine.

Her laptop was jangling madly as she headed back to the couch, wine in hand.

Flopping into the cushiony goodness, she propped her feet up on the coffee table and dragged her laptop in front of her, sipping the crisp pinot.

Jason's darkly handsome face appeared before her on the screen.

"Calling me straight back, goodness, I'm honored. Shouldn't you be out, romancing some young thing?"

His own glass came into view, as he toasted his wine towards her. "Cheers."

Nodding back, she raised hers. "Slainte."

He sipped his glass of red, giving her a croaky chuckle. "We're going Irish today, then? That's fitting." His voice trailed away before he suddenly realized what she'd said. "And no, in answer to your question, there is no 'young thing'. I'm giving them up."

Offering him an inelegant snort, she settled in for catch-up. He'd been her boss for five years, but her best friend much longer. "Oh really. Now that sounds like there's a story there. What's up?"

His usual smile faded as his gaze strayed to his own fire, and as he exhaled he relaxed back into his sofa, letting his guard down. His feelings of exhaustion and worry hit her like a bitter wind, and she leant closer to the screen, almost reaching out to him.

Snapping his stark blue gaze back to her, he shook his head, wrenching his hand back through his short dark hair.

"Jase, all this over a girl. What happened?"

There was no humor in his laugh. "It's not a girl. I wish it was—wish I'd had the time."

She looked out of her patio doors, watching the now bitterly cold rain fall in heavy splats. Just the thought of the drenching she'd get rushing up to London at this hour had her shivering, but she steeled herself against it, pushing to her feet. "I'm on my way—"

"No! No, gods, no. I'm not helpless, Jess, just let me blather on for a bit while I drink my wine, okay?"

He too had come to his feet to stop her flying out the door, and they both slowly eased back into their chairs.

"Okay, start talking. And, Buster, if I'm still worried I'm coming back tonight."

His pained chuckle and slight smile made her feel a little better.

He took a healthy swig of wine before taking a deep breath, like he was getting ready to run a marathon.

"Firstly, nothing is wrong with me. I've let someone down, and I think he might have been exposed because I didn't read the situation right."

"Exposed?" Jess pulled in a breath of her own. "How?"

"I sent him out on a valuation of what I'd assumed was a fake." He went quiet, his chin falling to his chest, and Jess heard all the things he wasn't saying.

"You mean you'd have normally sent me, just in case." His silence was all the answer she needed, and she wondered at the sanity of feeling guilty for needing to be with her family. "What was the artifact?"

The screen tipped from Jason's end as he jostled the laptop, trying to rub the headache from his temples. "I won't lie, Jess. I would've sent you, and it would've been *just in case*. But he's good, with a real eye, and I was so bloody certain it was a fake."

"Jason. By the goddess, tell me what it was!" Her heart was pounding in her chest; anxiety crawled up her spine. The unusual touch of fear had her gripping the laptop.

"It was the Ardagh Chalice."

Still leaning forward, she blinked, wondering if she'd heard him. "Ardagh?" She mentally flipped through her knowledge of European exhibitions. "It's a chalice... It's in Ireland, in Dublin at the National Museum. It's..." Her voice faded away as they stared at each other. Seventy miles sat between them, but she could feel the tension pouring from him as if he were in the room. "Jason?"

"It's not in the National Museum in Dublin—that's what I was doing there while you were in Rome. As I understand now, it's never been there."

Jess sat, waiting for the missing link in this chain of events.

"I got a random email, with photos of the chalice on dated newspapers, and some video footage. Even if it wasn't the Ardagh Chalice, the workmanship was spectacular. And it was old. Ancient. Maybe a duplicate—it's not the first time we've seen that sort of thing, is it?"

Grappling with her patience, Jess gritted her teeth. It's a good job he was in London. Raising her eyes to the ceiling she took a deep breath, keeping her silence.

"Seb has a real gift with religious relics. He knew it was real the minute he laid eyes on it, and he knew they'd bolt if he tried to arrange a collection or exchange. So he wired the money straight over and left with it. In a bloody rucksack."

"Seb." She whispered his name as dread dropped through her. "You sent Seb because I was here in the bay?" Her voice cracked as guilt and fear filled her.

"No! Gods, no. It was before...when you were in Rome. That's why I sent him with you to the gala dinner. But I couldn't bloody get hold of you to explain why, because I had to fly to Ireland to learn more about the bloody poxy chalice."

"We were followed." Jess stared at him. "I thought it was me—but they were following him."

Jason went wholly still as she spoke. "When?"

"The night of the gala, we walked home through St. James's park." She swallowed the panic, her mind racing a mile a minute. "I know there's all kinds of things wandering around London, but they don't usually bother me. I just assumed something foolish had picked up my signature."

"What happened?"

"I, uh...a mirror spell gave it a shock. But it tracked us to the hotel, where I sent it on its way. Hard."

Releasing his held breath he rubbed his brow. "'Jesus, Jess, mirror magic! How did you keep Seb from seeing?"

She lifted her glass, taking more of a gulp than a sip. "It all just fell into place. I'd hoped I'd given it enough of a warning... Has it come back?"

Jason shrugged. "I don't know. The chalice is locked up at the museum, but it must have a powerful pull. It's drawing all sorts to it, so I've called in a favor and had the protection spells here amped up."

Dread ballooned, the sound of her shallow breaths filled her head. "What is the chalice?"

"It's purported to have re-animative qualities. Hence the reason it isn't in the Dublin Museum where it's supposed to be. Filled with the right substance it can rejuvenate a husk."

Jess stilled, hysterical laughter bubbling up within her. "A husk? You mean a dead vampire?"

All that greeted her was his silence.

Her mouth dried out as she looked at him. "I thought they'd just about died out." Her words sounded foolish, she knew, fundamentally, that anything could survive as long as it could hide within the boundaries of humanity. All they had to do was feign civility, and mankind did that every day.

"Seb left Scotland with it, and travelled for a day and a half with the chalice on his person. Anyone with any kind of radar for power or old energy will have picked it up. And his scent with it. That's the second time he's had a near miss, and he has no idea what he's done."

Jason's image jerked from the screen as he came to his feet, pent-up rage and fear forcing him to move. She watched as he placed the laptop on the table and began to pace. His voice coming in and out.

"I've found every reason possible to keep him either at the Museum or with me, but the exhibition opens Friday, and I need you here. You'll pick up outside energy much quicker than I will. Can you find some way to cloak him—or strip him of the chalice's imprint?"

Jess shook her head, trying to silence the roaring panic in her brain so she could think. "That kind of spell craft just isn't in my wheelhouse, and you know that interfering with humanity always has a backlash. That's why I didn't cloak him before I left, it would just raise the magical stamp on him."

She too began to pace, discarding ideas as she worked them through. "You say this is his second near miss with the esoteric world?"

She heard ice hit crystal before he came back into focus, with a large scotch in hand. "Yeah. He was in Canada a few months back, they had one hell of a snow storm and he had a run in with a *loup-garou*."

"A *loup-g*...a werewolf. Jeez, Jase, why not just call it a werewolf?"

"*Loup-garou* are wild, completely wild—not like lyke. This one must've fed recently, as from what I can gather, all he did was give Seb a hell of a fright. He phoned me from the hospital, in Canada. He was pretty delirious, and drugged up." Releasing a sigh he shook his head. "By the time I got to him a day later, he was his usual self, saying the cold had disoriented him." Jason went back to sipping his scotch.

Focusing her thoughts, she tried to push her worry for Seb to the back of her mind. She'd never be able to think clearly with panic clambering to take hold. "Fate has her hand in this, Jason. Surely you can see that? You can't swim against the tide of what is meant. Fate will find a way to get what it wants. We just need to figure out what that is. Do you think he's being hunted?"

"I don't know." The urgency in his voice sent shivers skittering up her spine. "Jess, he's my friend. I know we can't alter fate, but we can try to skew events in our favor... So what *can* we do?"

She grabbed the laptop and put it up on the kitchen side. "Okay." She took a deep breath, briefly closing her eyes to quieten her mind. "Okay." She moved a book that she'd left out, sliding it back onto the shelf, straightening others while she was there.

As she rolled different choices around, following the actions through, trying to guesstimate possible outcomes, Jason spoke. "The chalice will only be here for another three days. By Saturday evening it will be on its way, heading somewhere safe and secure."

Just because the chalice would no longer be their problem, didn't mean anything for Sebastian.

"I could clear the chalice; it might stop the strength of its emanation. Which *might* muddy the waters." She pursed her lips as she looked at Jason.

"I could do the same for him—clear his etheric field, but goddess knows how we'd explain it. It's not something that would work without his consent."

She leant back against the worktop, crossing her arms. "You know as well as I do, that any kind of magical signature will mark him. And a human walking around London, with knowledge of our world—no matter how small—will make him fair game. We can't do that to him."

Closing the laptop she curled up on the sofa, laying her head on hands as she stared into the fire.

Jason had been her best friend since school, she always wondered if they'd recognized that there was something *other* about themselves. And even as a teenager, when he was growing into making his first full change, she'd never seen him this agitated.

He'd gone straight to work at the museum when she'd gone to uni, and he'd worked every hour, proving his worth. When he'd begun the prestigious role of heading up the Exhibitions Department for the Victoria and Albert Museum, he'd brought her on board.

She'd studied constantly. Trying to make sure her knowledge of the industry was solid. She'd always felt a little uncomfortable with having a gifted advantage; being able to read the relics just by touching them.

Over the last three years, their department at the Museum had become a little more select, and although they still managed exhibitions all over the world, they were handy backup for the authorities in cases of historical art theft and fraud.

She often ended up appraising bits of junk in dirty back rooms, for questionable clientele. But he didn't have to worry about her.

Jason had made it his business to isolate the more dangerous items, seeing them out of harm's way—out of human way. And she'd ended up as some kind of comic side-kick, crazily backing his crusade.

But things were different now. Seb was clearly important to Jason, and in the blink of an eye he'd become important to her.

CHAPTER 6

As the train pulled into Waterloo, Jess stayed in her seat. Worry warred with glee at being back in her city after so long away. The Island and London were opposite sides of the same coin for her, both making up the whole.

She calmed her breathing, waiting for the crowds to disembark. She made sure she was always a straggler. It was safer to let the river of energy flow around her.

All their thoughts, fears and joy mixed together, was easier to work with than a direct hit of random positive or negative.

Thea had been so afraid when Jess had first said she'd wanted to study in London.

Jess knew how much Thea had struggled with the London crowds. But even before Thea had become the strong, self-protected woman she was now, that hadn't stopped her traveling up, and checking in on her little sister.

As she watched a sleepy commuter double-wrap his scarf against the icy wind, she slowly came to her feet, following him from the train, smiling at thoughts of her family.

The people before her became a colorful flow of energetic

life; a mishmash of emotion that rippled across her, like the snare drum on a jazz track.

She fed her ticket into the reader on the turnstile, and the arm rotated to let her off the platform and into Waterloo Station.

The large Victorian clock monitored time, silently.

The dozens of display boards updated train times. Pigeons idled across the white stone floor, muddling around feet and luggage.

The beeps and rings of text alerts, emails and phone calls echoed off of the brick and metal, lifting into the steel girders and bouncing from the glass ceiling.

She drifted left, following the mass, joining the thrum, heading for the ever downward spiral of the underground.

The warm, damp air rushed up at her.

Jess pulled her Jackie Ohh's from her coat pocket, shielding her eyes, as even contact lenses wouldn't be able to cover her reaction. The escalator ran flat as she stepped on it. She loved the moment it tipped over the edge, easing down into the tunnels.

People, like statues, stood before her, as the giant mechanical beast rolled endlessly.

Colorful line maps and a maze of corridors led her to the tube.

She grasped the yellow handrail, and swayed with the motion of the carriage.

There was a certain point when the air changed and the silence crackled, that filled Jess with excitement.

The glittering sensations travelled through her body and settled in the pit of her stomach, radiating waves of anticipation. The fine hairs on the back of her neck shivered and licked at her nerve endings, and the urge to giggle lodged in her throat as she looked at the glum faces of the people surrounding her.

They were crowded in every available space, bumping and jostling each other as the underground train lurched towards Embankment.

Feeling the train shudder to a halt, she allowed herself to be taken along with them; off the train, and through the tunnels and passageways, that would lead her up to the dark streets of London.

Her blood screamed around her system, pouring through her body, morphing to a roar in her ears. She felt her patience slipping beyond her control.

As she came to the dark street she wrenched her sunglasses off, pulled left away from the crowd as they surged up and out.

The wonderful smell of rain and the chill night air slid through her, as she came to a brief standstill.

As the hordes around her disappeared off into the night, she savored this moment, heading towards the Thames, feeling its very essence in her blood. Her breath was coming in fast pants as she came closer to the water.

It was well after 1am, and although the city was never truly silent, the bitterly cold, wet Thursday in October was driving the final few loners from the streets, and for just a small portion of time, this stretch of the city was hers.

The dark, fog-filled night became a comforting blanket that wrapped around her, protecting her from prying eyes.

Darting in and out of side streets her feet barely touched the ground, until finally she came upon the river.

The light from the London Eye was glinting at her from across the water, the heavy damp was lying thick on the trees, and the age old scent of time laced the air.

Her feet became rooted to the spot as the vibrations from around her sent images and sounds flashing through her mind; all the people and all the noise. The cars, buses and boats that had travelled throughout the day crawled into her system.

Jess remained completely still, as did the night around her.

Her body began to fill with latent energies, her long dark hair rippled, coming up and away from her back.

She knew the deep brown of her eyes had already begun to fade, as the unearthly lavender eclipsed them.

Pulling in a heaving breath, her exaggerated sensory perception registered every sound, every movement around her. And safe in the knowledge that she was completely alone she let her arms hang down at her sides, and splayed her fingers in a sharp motion that lifted her from the ground.

Offering a quick whisper to the stars to protect her from prying eyes, she released a surge of power and hurtled at breakneck speed along the water's edge—reveling in the scents and sounds of her beloved city.

The long dark tresses of her hair fanned out, and the vibrations from her palms eased her higher. The excitement ripped and jerked through her system as she cleared the tops of the trees along the embankment.

She arched towards the water darting between the trees, and flicked her delicate hands, hurling herself through the frigid air, her hair whipping out behind her.

Jess stared at the ceiling as she waited for the 6am alarm to sound. It was still dark. The sound of the wind had her stifling a shiver as she yawned and crawled from her toasty bed.

She grabbed a hairclip from the dresser and, twisting her hair as high up as she could, she pinned it into submission.

Staring at herself in the mirror, she smoothed her hands across her cheeks, wishing she'd caught even a glimmer of the summer sunshine to ease her pale complexion through the first of the winter weeks. Her dark eyes, brows and hair left her skin looking a bit ghostly, and a sleepless night hadn't helped.

The text-vibration of her phone announced that Jason was going to collect breakfast for the three of them, and forcing down her weird nerves, she texted him back.

Pinching her cheeks, she headed for the shower, mentally rummaging through her wardrobe as she went.

The hot water hit her back, making her groan and stretch at the same time. She leaned forward as she washed, trying as much as possible to save her hair from a dowsing. She was in no mood to deal with a blow-dry this morning.

Shutting off the shower, she grabbed a towel, catching her hair as it slid from its precarious position, heading for her bedroom.

Make-up helped to cover the worst of the shadows beneath her eyes, and the loose plait that hung over her shoulder softened her face.

Stopping at the bedroom window she cast an eye out at the dreary rain. The short walk to the Museum was going to be a damp one.

Zipping up her worn-in brown long boots over her skinny jeans, she pulled a blazer from the wardrobe just to smarten it up. She was doubtlessly going to be in a dusty archive or crawling around the storage department today, but still, she didn't want to look messy.

Ignoring the snort of her little voice, she tossed a few things in her shoulder bag and headed out.

The October rain hadn't taken on the full chill of winter yet, but it was in the air. The traffic was already in full London mode as she turned onto Cromwell Street.

As she passed the entrance to the Rembrandt she glanced down the side alley, wondering if Jason could hunt out a trace of whatever it was that she'd sent hurtling down there a few weeks back. Even just a faint idea would give them something to go on.

Pressing the light on the crossing junction, she sighed. She really should have thought of that sooner. The pouring rain of the last few weeks had surely wiped it out by now.

Dashing across the road she headed to the front entrance of the Museum, offering smiles and good mornings as she went.

The energy around here felt different, and she wondered whom Jason had called in to beef up their metaphysical security.

Knowing that taking the elevator would be quicker, she chose the stairs, trying to decide what on earth she was going to say to Seb.

Pushing through the door into their little HQ, she didn't get a chance to decide as she all but mowed Jason down.

Barely able to save his coffee, he grinned at her, the relief in his blue eyes palpable. "Jess. Nearly floored ya. You okay, babe? How's Adam?"

Stifling a surprised laugh she loosed the death grip she had on her shoulder bag, hanging it on the coat rack. "Hey. He's okay, daft bugger that he is."

Turning in search of the breakfast, she found Seb's dark gaze locked on her. He sat at one of the desks, coffee in hand. She was saddened to see his lack of a suit today—not that he should be wearing one, but when you wear something that well...

She sighed at the thought. Still, he was looking fine in a navy sweater, and what looked like a soft shirt underneath and dark jeans. Just fine indeed.

Filching a pastry from the box, she poured herself a coffee and offered him a smile. "Sebastian."

His slight smile in response only lifted one corner of his lips, as dipped his head in acknowledgment. "Jessica." He said her name slowly, just the sound of his voice had excitement tingling through her. "Everything okay now?"

There was a wealth of unsaid words in the few he spoke. Jess pulled up a chair to sit opposite him, killing time faffing about.

"Yeah. All good. Just crazy family stuff."

She could feel Jason's eyes boring into her as he watched them. If she got even a whiff of his hand matchmaking in this she'd be fine-tuning her transmutation abilities, and he'd find himself learning how to live life as a little Chihuahua or Lhasa Apso.

As if reading her mind, she arched her brow at him, Jason stifled a grin and motivated himself.

"Okay then." His overly cheerful tone wasn't lost on her as he grabbed his laptop and pulled up a chair with them. "Lots to do. The Gods and Worship gallery opens tomorrow night, and we've just about got everything in place, all it needs now

is unpacking, fine touching and the like."

Taking notes as Jason ran through what would be an unspeakably hectic two days, she glanced at Seb, who was doing the same.

Jason was clearly handing babysitting duties over to her, as she'd been assigned every task with him in tow. She wondered if he'd noticed yet that he wasn't getting five minutes to himself.

"And I've got investor meetings today, but I'll be on hand tomorrow, if that works for you both?"

"Sure thing." Jess nodded as she stood, heading for her office.

"Oh Jess, this exhibition has been stepped up, and tomorrow night is black tie."

Pushing open her office door, she threw a 'Sure, sure,' over her shoulder, stopping dead in her tracks at the piles of mail sitting on her desk.

"Oh, that's a nice welcome back." Seb's voice tickled her nerves as he stood close behind her, his heat sinking into her back.

Taking her time moving away from the lovely warmth of him, she latched the office door open, turning. "Yup. How have you found the last few weeks?" The polite conversation was so at odds with all the things she wanted to ask him.

Leaning back against the sash window in her office, he crossed his arms over his chest, "Truth? Jason's kept me too busy to notice." Waiting a beat, he flashed her a grin. "But I'm glad you're back, if that's what you're asking."

Arching a brow at him, she gave him a solemn nod. "I'll bet. Need help with the workload, do ya?" Her slight smirk ruined the effect.

"Yeah sure, of course *that's* why I'm glad your back."

Rifling through the mail on her desk, she let that remark slide as she made a pile of junk mail for the shredder. She'd hoped he'd be pleased to see her. She'd also hoped that maybe he'd thought better of this *thing* between them, and would save her from her having to call it to a halt. Which was a pain in the ass in itself, as she was fairly sure that her willpower was not going to be her strong point when it came to a tall, brown-eyed historian who reminded her of the sea and tasted like fine whisky.

Maybe if she got it out of the way, quick... But as she looked up, he'd already started to head for the door.

"If you're going to be busy for half hour, I'll clear my emails before we head down to the exhibition."

Closing her mouth, she tightened her fingers around the letters in her hand.

She'd almost done it then, she'd been, like, so close.

Of course you were.

She rolled her eyes, already sick of her little voice. "Okay, I'll give you a knock when I'm done."

Stopping at the door, he held her gaze, making her stomach do flips as she waited.

"Jess," he cleared his throat, "it really is good to see you."

Dropping the mail to her desk, she slid her hands in her pockets, raising her shoulders. "You too. Although I don't think—"

Holding his hands up, he backed away with a wink. "Your being glad to see me is enough. For now."

He murmured the final words like a promise as he turned away, and, sitting down at her desk, Jess knew she was already in hot water. A few weeks away had only intensified the chemistry between them.

～

AS HE ALTERED the angle of a marble bust of Medusa, he watched her chat with one of the staff, pointing out changes she'd like made and checking if it could be done.

The soft blue denim fit her like a second skin, curving beautifully across her thigh and up, over her perfect derriere. She'd left her blazer up in the office, and the black top brushed her hips. The plait hanging over her shoulder gave her the look of a student, and it was hard to believe that she was the 26 years that Jason had confirmed.

He was biding his time until he could get her alone, taste her lips and prove to himself they couldn't possibly be as soft as he remembered. She'd lived in his thoughts the whole time she'd been gone.

He found it disturbing that she'd been able to slip into his mind and stay there after one night. Whether they worked together or not, he had to find out what this thing was between them.

Moving on to the next display, he mentally acknowledged that getting the time and privacy at the moment would be a problem. Jason had kept his work and social calendar constantly full since he'd gotten back from Ireland. There'd been dinners and fundraisers, late nights with the exhibition; he'd even temporarily moved into Jason's spare room as he just hadn't had time to look for a flat, and living out of a hotel room had lost its shine—fast.

Drawn out of his thoughts at the sound of her laughter, he watched her assuring her helper that she could manage as he had 'enough to do.' As she turned away consulting her iPad, she reassured her assistant that she was perfectly capable of going to the archive herself.

Casting his eyes at all the bodies currently working on this exhibition, he figured the archive was most likely to be empty...

Giving her a few minutes head start, he strolled slowly after her.

Letting the door close softly behind him, he breathed in the comforting smells of musty paper and ancient text, as she bent over the table, the bright spotlight shining down on the page.

"Hey." His low whisper had her looking up, heat touching her high cheekbones. "I wondered when I was going to be able to steal five minutes with you."

Her brown eyes widened as he approached her, as she clearly searched for the right way to put him off. Her tongue dabbed her top lip as she readied herself to speak, but she was already too late.

Catching her hips, he stepped against her, her breath leaving her in a rush as he pulled her to him, firmly.

Her eyes darted up to his, and her hot breath rushed across his lips, as her hands fisted on his chest.

"Seb, I..."

Leaning down to the soft skin between her shoulder and her neck he breathed her in. Never had he enjoyed the smell of a woman so much.

"You...?" Careful not to mark her, he scraped his jaw up the skin of her neck, loving the feel of the shiver moving through her as his whiskers rubbed her.

The faintest sound left her lips as she tilted her head, exposing more of her alabaster skin.

Heartened by her response, he slid his hands further, grasping the round cheeks of her ass, lifting her snugly to him, pressing his hard length against the soft, warm heat of her.

Kneading the soft cheeks, he captured her moan with his lips, as he took her mouth, his hunger overwhelming. Blood pounded to his shaft, as she moved softly in his grasp. His reaction to her floored him.

Sweeping through the recess of her lush mouth, the taste of her was bliss, her tongue matching his own need.

Lifting her onto the desk, he pushed between her thighs, jerking her back where he needed her.

Grasping her hips to keep her close, he ground into her. Her soft gasp matching his low groan.

He feasted on her lips, her whispered moans urging him closer, making him lose track of time and place, as he stood between her spread legs.

The faint sound of voices in the corridor had him cupping her jaw, taking one last sweet sip from her, before pulling his lips away.

She rested her brow against his chest, her thighs still gripping his hips, as she breathed slowly, and the footsteps continued on by.

Taking a few calming breaths himself, he looked down at the top of her head, her glossy hair reflecting under the light, as he rubbed his palms up and down her thighs. "Jess. I...uh, I didn't mean for it to get so...to go so...you know?"

Her muffled laughter reached him, as she took a final deep breath, raising her gaze to his. "I know. And I'm supposed to be explaining to you why *this* isn't a good idea."

Her self-deprecating smile erased his tinge of guilt for pushing her. "And you're doing a fine job of it... Now tell me again why what isn't a good idea?"

"Sebastian." Pushing at his hips she wriggled from his embrace, hopping off the table. "You *know* why. We work together. Jason is a mutual friend. We *work* together, blah blah." Pacing away from him, she waved her hand as she spoke, before stopping to glare pointedly at him with her hands on her hips. "You can't tell me you think this," she gestured between the two of them, "is a sensible idea?"

Crossing his arms over his chest, he shook his head, fingers of anger teasing at him. "Oh, screw sensible, Jess." Pacing towards her, he scraped his hand through his hair. "Life is too short for *sensible*. You make me hot. And I mean *hot.*" Pulling her back against him so she could feel how aroused he was, he brought his face a dash away from hers. "You make me laugh, and I can't seem to get you out of my mind. Why would I ignore that just to be *sensible*?"

He flung the words at her, but his hands were gentle as they rubbed over her lower back, softly coaxing her. "Now I admit, *here* may not be the best place to have this discussion."

"You can say that again." Her inelegant snort chased the flash of anger away.

And his voice softened as he spoke. "But you can't ignore it, Jess."

As she released her pent up breath, he brushed his lips over hers.

Groaning, she pushed him away. "This is where we got into

trouble in the first place!" Holding her palm up as if to keep him at bay, she pointed at him with her other hand. "Maybe there is *something* going on between us, but it can't be here—"

"Agreed." Butting in before she could offer any other delaying tactics, he opened his palms at her as she looked suspiciously at him. "I do—I agree. Not here. So have dinner with me?"

As she rolled her eyes, he could feel her reserve breaking. "We've got the exhibition launch tomorrow night, and it's going to be mental after that. So tonight?"

He could see it in her eyes, she wanted to say yes, but she was clinging to that last little niggle of 'sensible and logical.'

"We could go straight from work—it's not like we're going to get out of here early anyway—we don't even have to call it a date if that helps you to kid yourself." He winked at her as he said it, watching the humor race across her face, before she threw her hands in the air.

～

"FINE. DINNER." Rolling her eyes, she breezed past him, switching off the spotlight that still glared down at the document as she went.

Dammit. She'd let him work her over, she'd let herself be led along. Because despite all the reasons that this was a bad idea, there was something about him and her together.

Falling into step beside her, he dropped his arm across her shoulders.

She suppressed the urge to grin, knowing he was deliberately trying to bait her.

Shrugging off his arm, she gave him what she hoped was her best pointed stare. "And you can cut that out too. What's gotten into you?"

Shaking his head, he rolled his shoulders. "Beats me. You must bring it out in me."

Opening her mouth to inform him he was responsible for his own moods, she snapped it shut when he said, "What do you fancy for dinner?"

It felt like such a mundane question, a couple's kind of question. Nerves, that had nothing to do with his proximity, tripped through her system. She liked him—she liked the way he looked, sure, there was nothing not to like. But she liked *him,* the way he made her feel; the way she felt like she'd known him forever. Being with him was so easy.

But she wasn't ready for mundane. For discussing dinner and setting alarms, doing the same thing. Everyday. Over and over again.

Long forgotten nerves dropped through her.

"Dinner." Stopping dead in her tracks, she touched her forehead. "I totally forgot, I'm already out." Turning away, she headed towards the stairs that would take her to her office. "I've just got to get some papers, I'll be back down in a bit."

Striding away, she raced up the stairs, glad to find the offices empty.

She shut her door and leaned back against it, taking a calming breath.

Jess knew she was overreacting. She'd probably confused the hell out of him, bearing in mind she'd just been wrapped round him like a trailing vine.

Embarrassment flooded her as heat filled her cheeks. Talk about sending mixed signals. Grabbing the pile of junk mail, she went into the main office, flipping the switch on the shredder.

Staring out of the window, she idly pushed each letter through the grinding teeth, enjoying the noise as it stripped each piece.

It wasn't that she didn't want a relationship, eventually, one day. Maybe.

It just wasn't on her agenda right now. She liked her own space, calling her own shots. And what about who she was? Did she really expect him to just take her magic in his stride?

A little flirting was one thing, but she'd spent *one day* with him, and she'd *missed* him every day since.

The heavy ball of nerves took up residence low in her stomach.

She was no good to anybody hiding up here in the office, and even though he was safe for the moment, surrounded by the busy bustle of the museum, that wouldn't protect him tonight.

Jason was relying on her to keep him at work late, until he could get back, and now she'd just bloody said she had plans. *Bugger it.* Because she'd been afraid, and her first response had been to run.

After watching the last envelope get drawn to its doom, she turned the shredder off, and rolled her shoulders. Straightening her stance, she replaced the lipstick that he'd kissed away and headed back down the exhibition. It was time to woman-up.

As she reached the bottom of the steps the precise strains of Chopin drifted from the open doors.

Sebastian was moving between each artifact, dimming and lifting the lighting. Shadows lay across the highly polished floor, cast by light on marble and pewter, glass and gold.

The serenely calming energy that was supposed to fill a museum was coming to life around her. Despite there still be packing crates and empty pedestals here and there, a sense of time and stillness was slowly breathing to life.

Leaning against the doorframe, she watched as he stood before each piece, waiting. He was taking in each position, moving between the displays. Every so often he'd stop, leaving a note on an empty stand—doubtlessly, he'd decided what should go there.

He'd taken his jumper off, and rolled up the sleeves of the soft white and blue checked shirt. His jeans fit perfectly, the cotton pulled across his shoulder blades, his thick hair just brushing his collar.

His easy grace was like a dance, his eye for detail was as good as her own, and with a sigh Jess approached him.

She'd never been a coward, and now wasn't a time to start.

"Hey." Her voice was hushed—the room demanded it. "Chopin?"

Turning to her, there was no ready smile, just a curious expression as he studied her. "Yes. Music helps an exhibition; it stops the silence."

"It's looking outstanding." Sliding her hands into the pockets of her jeans, she held his gaze. "You have a wonderful eye."

"Thank you." He tilted his head as he looked her. "What's the matter, Jess?"

"I cancelled my plans tonight. There's still a lot to do here," she gestured towards the back of the room, "but we could get Chinese delivered if you wanted to?"

CHAPTER 7

MOUTH-WATERING aromas of beef in black bean, egg fried rice and noodles wound up the stairs with her.

She'd ripped into the bag of prawn crackers as soon as the delivery driver had been safely locked out, and she crunched her way through her second one as she entered the office.

Jess had balanced the box of food precariously on one arm, finding Seb rummaging through what was loosely classed as their only kitchen cupboard, coming out with two odd-sized pub wine glasses.

"How is it that you have wine in the fridge but not a plate in the place?"

Laughing at him, she slid the box onto the table. "I think that says very positive things about us, to be fair." She pinched another prawn cracker from the packet and pulled boxes and tubs from the box. "On the other hand, you won't find enough plates in this whole place to dish up the amount of Chinese you ordered. There's enough for ten people here!" Her voice rose as she continued unpacking, digging around for the chopsticks, and handing him a set.

"I was hungry, and I didn't know what you wanted."

Stuffing the chopsticks in his back pocket, he reached up onto the top shelf. "Here's a bowl; it's the best I can do."

Wrinkling her nose at the earthenware bowl she turned solemn eyes on him. "At least there's wine."

Drawing a cold bottle of white from the fridge, he nodded, laughing. "Point taken."

Holding up their two glasses, she watched him pour, his large hand wrapped firmly around the bottle, and she just about stopped herself from moving a step closer to him, wanting to soak up his warmth.

The day had been lost in a snap as they'd worked side by side. She'd never really worked *with* anyone else, where they made equal decisions; it was interesting how similar their methods were. "We got a lot done today."

Taking his wine, his fingers brushed hers, as he tilted his glass towards her. "We did. We work well together."

Tapping her glass to his, she sipped the cool liquid, enjoying the brief heat of his skin.

"We do." Sitting down in the office chair, she peeled off lids, letting the gorgeous smells fill the room. "Ohmygods, I'm starving." Snapping her chopsticks apart she nabbed a piece of chicken, loving the spicy heat. "Nothing this bad should smell so good."

Loading food into his bowl, he sat down. "Same." He leant back in his chair, half a chicken ball still held in his fingers. "The office won't smell great tomorrow, though."

"True enough, but it's worth it."

Making short work of the tiny portion in her truly small bowl, she dragged the noodles across the table towards her, twirling them around her chopsticks. "Can you cook?"

Squinting his eyes at her with a grin, he swallowed his mouthful. "Why? You vetting skill-sets for my potential?"

Snickering around the slippery chow mein, she grabbed a

napkin, dabbing her lips. "Nah. Just asking. You see, you look like you should be able to cook."

Sipping his wine, he nodded towards her. "I do? What does that *look* like?"

"You know, you look...healthy. You look like you run or cycle. You drank water all day today—no coffee. So you're health conscious. You've got fruit on your desk..." She drifted to a stop at his look. "What?"

"I didn't realize you were paying such close attention." Leaning forward, he topped up her wine, setting the bottle down so he could catch her plait, gently tugging her to him. "Anything else you noticed?" His lips were soft as they caught hers, teasing her bottom lip with his tongue before nipping it with his teeth.

Grasping the arms of her office chair, he wheeled her to him, her jean-clad legs fitting between his.

Resting her palms on his hard thighs, she leant into him, and carefully taking his lip in return, she swept her tongue across it, testing the softness.

Coming to his feet, he pulled her to hers, his tongue sweeping past her lips. His grip became urgent as he grasped her hips, lifting her, and she wrapped her legs around him.

The last of her thoughts, before they all fled, was how quickly this was all getting out of hand.

Jess felt his hard length press against that soft, heated part of her. She knew she was lost as he turned for the couch.

The slamming door at the bottom of the stairs had her pulling away, her wide-eyed gaze looking into his equally shocked ones. How many times could they be interrupted?!

Rapidly unlacing her legs from his hips she slid to the floor, putting some space between them, as Jason's voice echoed up the stairwell.

"Hey, you two still here?"

She rolled her eyes. He bloody knew they were. She'd

totally forgotten that he was coming, and she briefly offered thanks that at least he was early. Or gods knew what he'd have walked in on.

Brushing herself down, she went back to her seat, just picking up her wine as Jason pushed into the room, a huge pizza box in his hand.

"I brought pizza, didn't know if you'd—" He stopped talking as he took in the Chinese, and Jess took a too large gulp of wine at the slight twinkle in his eye as he looked at them. Oh yeah, he knew alright.

"You two not hungry for pizza then?"

Leveling a glare at him, she picked up a chicken ball, knowing it was safer to keep her mouth busy.

Grabbing another glass from the cupboard, Seb reached for the wine gesturing at Jason. "Yes?"

Dropping the box to the table, he took off his rucksack and jacket. "Absolutely. Just let me put this stuff in my office."

Seb poured his wine, setting it down on the table, and leant over Jess as the office door slammed shut behind Jason. Holding her chin, he took her lips in a hard kiss.

"You won't get away next time."

His voice was a rough bur across her lips, and her stomach clenched at the heavy look in his eyes, as heat pooled low.

Seb had just taken his seat as Jason emerged from his office.

Wishing she knew just how good Jason's exaggerated sense of hearing was, she merely looked at his questioning gaze, as he gave her an overly innocent smile, before pulling up a chair.

"So, how's it been? Did you get much done?"

Passing his wine over, she flipped back the lid on the pizza box, and let the amazingly glutinous smells of takeaway mix together.

"We're just about done—a few details left to guide the interns through tomorrow, I'd say. What about you?"

"Investors meetings bore the crap out of me, but what are you gonna do, you know?"

Picking up his glass, Seb smiled into his wine as Jason looked over at him.

"Don't grin at me, my friend. What with all the funding you secured for the University I may tag you in."

Glancing around Jason to Jess, he gave her a serious look. "Did I tell you that I could find another museum to take my skills?"

Playing along, she picked up her wine. "Really? Do you think they'd have space for one more?"

Swallowing the enormous mouthful of pizza, Jason glared at the pair of them. "Yeah right, you'd both be miserable anywhere else; neither of you are anywhere near stuffy enough. And besides, none of the other museums in this city keep Chateauneuf-du-Pape next to the coffee machine."

Laughing and nearly choking on her last mouthful of noodles, she swallowed, wiping her watering eyes with her napkin. "You fool. Come on, grab a piece of pizza and come down to the exhibition hall. You can at least work if you're going to insult us."

Handing the remote control to Seb, she pushed open the gallery doors, as he activated the lighting and the music. Chopin's dreamy chords drifted through the softly lit gallery, light glinted, reflecting, forming angles of light and dark.

Life-size sculptures of Greek gods looked down upon the gold and silver offerings that were forged and beaten in their honor.

Ancient time hazed all around, almost tangible it was so strong. Shouts of slaves, and the rhythmic sound of a chisel striking marble echoed through her.

The sun had long since set; the silence of the night-time

heightened the stillness, and she looked in wonderment at how much they'd accomplished in a few short hours.

Jason and Seb moved through, murmuring back and forth. Seb's maple hair caught the light, in direct contrast to the dark black sweep of Jason's. They most likely wrought havoc when they were out together, both of them being tall and charming.

Tutting under her breath, she consciously wiped the frown from her features, unamused by her unusual flash of jealousy. He was a free agent, and so was she.

Not that she'd date two men at once. Not that she'd been dating anyone. Rolling her eyes at her own crazy self, she shook off the unexpected thoughts, moving towards them.

"It's looking good, isn't it?"

Jason turned to her. "Jess. It's looking bloody marvelous, I honestly thought it would be close to the wire." Making a sweeping gesture all around them, he laughed. "But this... this leaves all of us time to actually get ready for the opening, maybe even have a drink first."

Throwing Seb a wink she nodded in agreement. "Now you're talking. I know this great whisky bar that you've just got to try."

Rolling guilty blue eyes at her he darted his gaze back to Seb. "You didn't?"

Jabbing Jason in the arm, she crossed her arms and huffed at him. "Jason MacIntyre. I ought to fry your circuits. That place was gorgeous."

Giving her a wide-eyed look, Jason laughed, ribbing her in return. Seb seemed to not notice her slip about zapping her best friend, and she let the joke roll as they stood in the center of the exhibition hall. The huge vaulted ceiling above them, catching her laughter as it lifted to the rafters.

"Come on, Jess, you know I wouldn't leave you out." Lifting his brow at her, he held his palms wide in truce. "I've been on the waiting list for membership for months, and I got accepted while you were in Greece."

Uncrossing her arms, she gave him a friendly pat on the arm. She dragged out the "Okay," with a saccharine smile of forgiveness. "I suppose I should feel a little bit guilty, then..." straightening up the name tag on a gold chalice, she gave them both an exaggeratedly innocent look, "...for letting Seb convince me that putting our night out on your tab would make me feel better."

Seb's shout of laughter was punctuated by Jason's groan as he looked between his two friends. "Holy gods, I'm probably broke with the expensive taste you two have."

Seb slapped his shoulder as they walked through the gallery. "Don't worry, buddy, hers was cheaper than mine."

Jason rolled his eyes as Jess switched off the lights and music, muttering, "Small comfort."

Only the low level security lighting remained on as they walked a few steps ahead while she pulled the huge doors closed, and slid the latch into place. Their laughter carried back to her as they reached the reception hall.

Her footsteps echoed on the marble as she went to catch them, reverberating across the floor into the hall as a chill raced across her shoulders.

Slowly coming to halt, she turned a full circle, peering down the corridors around her, into the darkness, searching for the source of the icy fear that coursed through her veins.

"Jess." Seb stopped, looking back at her, a curious expression on his face. "You coming?"

Locking eyes with Jason, she knew with a cold certainty that they were too late. "Run!"

The shout had barely left her lips as the gothic window above them imploded, the ear-splitting noise like a lightning bolt. Enormous shards of stained glass plummeted to the floor, shattering as it hit the ground.

"Jess!" Seb's frenzied shout had her spinning around as he ran towards her, his footfall scraping and crunching over the glass and debris. Pulling her to him, he sheltered her body as the glass rained down.

Frantically grabbing his belt, she swung him around, fighting to get out of his arms without hurting him, and pushed him behind her.

Jason skidded to halt beside them as she finally tore herself free, their arms outstretched, a barrier in front of Sebastian, as three leviathan figures hazed to corporeal form amongst the chaos.

The demonic churning of their red eyes was unlike anything Jess had ever seen, but as she glanced over at her friend she knew he had. His breathing deepened as his eyes glazed, turning an unearthly blue. His rage and hatred crackled from his skin as he focused on the beings.

"*Scourge.*" The word muffled like a growl as it left his lips.

She called softly to him, knowing the chances of him fighting the change weren't good. "Please, Jase. Let's get Seb *out of here!*" The low urgency in her voice was slowly reaching him, and his breathing labored as he fought for control.

Pushing between the pair of them, Seb grabbed her arm, trying to pull her behind him. "Jess, get back!"

Wrenching free, she threw her arm back across his body. "Not the time, Seb."

Jason's snarl vibrated along her nerve endings.

Seb's whispered, "*What the fuck...?*" was lost in the melee, as the largest of the three stepped forward.

"Give us the chalice, dog, and you will shed no blood tonight."

The other two were clearly desperate to attack, waiting for the command of their ring-leader. Long malicious fangs were visible as he spoke, and dread poured though her as she realized that any chance of keeping this hidden, of keeping Seb protected, was lost.

Letting her shoulders drop, she focused her power, pulling it from her core, channeling currents down her arms to her palms. Hiding her left hand behind Jason's back she lowered her right behind her, knowing that Seb would see the glowing as the power built, but the vampires wouldn't.

There was simply no time left; hiding her and Jason's *abilities* wouldn't mean anything if they all ended up dead. Nudging Jason, she touched his back, making sure he felt the static buzz of her magic, and would realize what she was up to.

"I will shed no blood." Turning his wild eyes on Jess, he looked from her back to the vampire. "But you won't be so lucky."

As Jason launched himself at the other two, Jess whipped her hands together, creating a single bolt of energy from her palms, hitting the ring-leader square in the chest.

His seemed to crumple, wrapping around the blow, as it launched him from the floor, flinging his broken body up, and back out into the night.

Turning briefly to look for Sebastian, she panicked to find him gone, as Jason roared for her to protect him.

Seb had raced into the frenzy, landing a solid blow on the second vampire, as Jason fought the third, but it wasn't enough.

Leaping to his feet, Jason pushed Seb clear, but as the other being grappled him to the ground, Jess knew he couldn't get to his friend in time.

Whispering the low chant beneath her breath, Jess used the spell to latch onto Seb's essence, whipping him up from the floor, out of the reach of the bloodthirsty creature heading straight for him.

Shaking loose his claws, Jason tore into the vampire at his

feet, ending him. Jess hurtled Seb towards Jason with a shout, "Jase! Get him out of here—to the safe room…" She flung the words over her shoulder as she zapped the last vampire.

She held him steady as the silvery-lilac beam snapped and hissed as it hit him. The electricity poured through him, burning. Smoke lifted around them as the creature roared, his red eyes seething with rage as he fought against her magic.

Catching Jason's eye in her peripheral vision, she shouted at him. "Jason…now!"

Seb careened into Jason at full force, knocking him to the floor, and as they both pushed back to their feet, Jason grabbed Seb's arm pulling him away, even as he fought back, shouting for Jess to follow them.

But his strength was no match for Jason in his half-turned form.

Yanking Seb across his shoulders, he leapt ten feet across the hall making for the stairs, taking them in huge bounds. As soon as they were out of sight, she closed her eyes, pulling everything she had within her, increasing the magic bursting from her palms.

With a horrendous scream, the vampire broke apart, and she propelled his ashen remains through the shattered window, out into the night.

Breathing hard, she ran for the control panel shutting off the security lighting, firing a bolt at the camera above the entranceway, shorting out the feed.

Planting her back firmly against the cold wall, she opened her palms.

> Any essence of vampire
> One, two, three,
> Remove them from my sanctuary.
> All evil will they brought here,
> Wipe it clean

Don't let it near.

She repeated the chant again, and then a third time, her voice echoing through the halls and chambers.

The charred and bleeding body of the remaining vampire fractured to dust, shifting; lifting from the ground it was pulled through the destroyed window high above the reception hall.

Releasing her pent up breath, Jess let her hands fall to her sides, taking in the carnage that lay all around. She'd need days to work up the kind of magic a spell of this magnitude would require, and time wasn't on her side.

She'd seen her first vampire tonight. And she'd used her magic to mortally wound. She couldn't find the horror for the first, or the guilt for the second. Faced with the same choices again, she'd take the same actions.

But her heart hurt at she stared down at the fragments of stained glass and lead. Hundreds of years of history, lost. The love and time of attentive craftsmen. A way of life that was no longer in existence, and could now no longer be studied.

But as she stared out into the night, that sadness faded in the face of what she knew was to come.

Setting her jaw, she pushed her tangled hair back from her face and headed over to the fire alarm box. On elbowing the glass, alarms began to scream around her, and she flung out her palms, pushing away from the floor, lifting out though the window, into the wind.

Hovering in the shadows, she whispered a protection spell, whirling the words into an intangible barrier across the shattered window, that would keep anything other than human from entering. The rebound spell would send them, with great force, back to where they came from.

Staying close to the building, her heart pounded as she made for the safe room.

CHAPTER 8

UNLATCHING THE WINDOW, Jason went to the hearth, striking a match and throwing it in. He stared at himself in the mirror above the fireplace, his eyes flickering from blue to black as he fought to get his beast in check.

Watching the fire as it crackled to life, he took slow, easy breaths, trying to release the rage that poured through the beast that prowled inside him.

Keeping a strained sigh to himself, he looked sadly away from his own reflection to that of the tightly angry man sat before him.

Jason had known Seb for years, his stubborn streak and complete self-belief had appealed to the hell-raiser in Jason, he'd liked that there was nothing stuffy about him, liked that he was always ready to laugh or go a few rounds at the bar.

As they'd worked together on and off different projects over the years, things had always come up like roses. He'd been so pleased to finally get him on staff for the museum, even tried his hand at matchmaking him with his best friend...

Jason took the seat facing Seb, easing himself back into the fireside chair, unsure of how to reach him.

~

THE RAIN HAD BEGUN to fall in earnest, lending a thickness to the silence.

The gentle glow of the wall lamp softly touched the red and burgundy hues of the room.

The leather fireside chair, warmed by the hearth, couldn't ease the tension twisting up through the muscles of his back and across his shoulders.

But despite his discomfort, Seb sat wholly still, refusing to give vent to the anger and frustration that seethed within him.

Raising his dark brown eyes, his gaze clashed with Jason's; it glowed with the menace of whatever lived within him.

Seb barely held on to his control. The cold rage settled over him like a blanket. He let his head fall back against the chair, releasing a choking sound—it could've been an attempt at a laugh, but it was devoid of all humor.

It was nothing more than self-aimed disgust; he'd followed blindly. Never once allowed the questions from the darkest depths of his mind to be voiced. He'd foolishly believed in the loyalty of their friendship.

He'd been a coward, hiding from things he'd hoped couldn't possibly be true.

"Seb. I know this is a lot to process."

He couldn't miss the tiredness in Jason's voice. Had seen the fear on his face as he'd shouted for Jess to protect him.

His brain viciously shut him down. He couldn't think about her right now. Couldn't think of the seething power coming from her hands, pouring through her slight frame.

He shook his head, fearing for his sanity.

"Process?" His voice scrapped over the word, as he levelled a flat stare at Jason. "All these years I thought you and I had trust. But you were just telling me what I wanted to hear. I *knew* there was more to you, to this whole set-up, but I just kept on letting things go by." His knuckles were white as he gripped the chair.

"I've let so many things go unnoticed. How many times have you just brushed things off? What about Canada? You *knew* that something had come after me; My mind so full of cold and death, certain that I'd been chased down by something more than a man. Did it come after me because of you?"

He flung the bitter accusation out, spewing rage like acid. "You let me wallow in my madness, used me, and sent me back out, to be hunted by god knows what."

~

JASON HELD his head between his hands, his groan was low and keening. He'd had no idea that Seb had picked up on him... Hadn't realized that he'd noticed so much.

He'd let him down—underestimated him. "Seb, I never lied—I didn't try and keep anything from you, I didn't..." The words died in his throat. He had used him, hadn't meant to. But that didn't matter now.

His decisions were costing him a friend, and he trusted so few that he wasn't prepared to just let Seb go.

Pushing to his feet, he battled the haze of anger still banging through his system, fighting to get his thoughts into a lucid state, to try and explain.

"Whatever happened in Canada...? I don't know why it came after you. When you called me from the hospital, I knew something was off—that's why I flew straight out. I wondered why you'd called me, wondered then if you could have possibly suspected. But by the time I arrived you were fine, you were *you* again; all easy-going. You said you'd been *lucky*!"

Jason pushed his hands into the pockets of his jeans, rolling his shoulders, trying to stretch out the tension, his tone exasperated. "You didn't give me any sign that you thought there was more to it! I would've tried to explain, to protect you!" He heard the blame in his voice, and knew that it wasn't going to solve anything.

Seb came to his feet in a rush, advancing on Jason. Any thought of danger lost in rage. "Christ! You're telling me I should be apologizing to you, for *not* mentioning that you're bloody strong. For *not* asking how you can hear people coming from *yards* away! What would you protect me from? You?!"

$\sim$

"THAT'S ENOUGH!"

"Jess." Seb whispered her name as he spun round at the sound of her voice, unconsciously taking a step towards her. Relief that she was unharmed rushed through him.

He stared at her; her plait had long ago come loose, and her dark hair was damp, windblown, hanging around her shoulders. The relief faded as he looked at her. How could her willowy frame harness so much power...?

She stood perfectly still, watching him with her back to the wood-paneled wall.

The door, he knew, was clear across the other side of the room.

He had no idea how many minutes they stood staring at each other. Her hands stayed still, hanging loosely at her sides.

She seemed to be waiting him out, waiting to see what he was going to do.

What was he going to do?

Her eyes were bright with emotion, swirling from deep, dark brown, to iridescent lavender. Realization struck as she looked at him, she didn't even attempt to shield her gaze from him now. She always hid her eyes when they'd kissed, she'd put her head on his chest, or turn away...

High color flagged her cheeks, and the dark top molded to her.

His heart sped up just from looking at her, and he cursed himself.

She looked past him, to Jason, her lips curled into a sad smile as she glanced between them. "Are you both okay?"

"I got him straight up here. Are you—?"

"How did you get in here?" Seb kept his gaze on her, cutting Jason off mid-flow. He moved towards her, stopping a few feet away.

Clearing her throat softly, she raised her hand, gesturing slowly behind her. "I came in through the window." The curtains hung wide and the rain lashed the unlatched pane.

Holding her hands out towards him, she took a tentative step forward. "Seb—"

He cut her off with a sharp shake of his head, as he looked from her and back to the window.

"We're three floors up. Don't expect me to believe you jumped. Now how did you get in here?"

His mind fought what she was trying to tell him, and he feared that he wouldn't be able to grasp it, that he'd just shatter, lost in a madness, thick like mud, drowning, and he'd be forever trying to claw his way out.

Her wide gaze returned to its normal warm brown, and tears shimmered. "I didn't jump." Her whispered words faded, as he whirled away.

"This is bullshit. I'm out." He wrenched the handle to leave, as Jason called to him.

"Seb, you're out alright—out of choices. You can leave now, but you're about to go walking around a city filled with beings that are *other*. For whatever reason you've been marked, and you'll be like a beacon calling them in. You're safer here—at least stay within the confines of the museum—these boundaries are protected."

~

JESS STUDIED HIM. His dark hair was wet, his usually playful eyes were full of confusion and distrust. "Please, Seb."

He hesitated briefly at her words. Then, giving Jason a sharp nod, he walked away.

The slamming door echoed around the room, and Jess felt her frame slacken as the air around her lost its charge.

She turned towards the window; virtually unable to stand any longer, she sat on the ledge and leaned back against the sash. The dark tumultuous night raging behind her was a perfect reflection of herself. Everything had changed in a click of time.

Staring down at the ground, her voice was quiet as she spoke. "I can't fix the rose window. But I got rid of the mess and the security footage. Then I set the alarms off." Not wanting to heap guilt on his already exhausted shoulders, but having to know, she asked, "I thought you'd upped the security?"

Rubbing at his forehead, he huffed in the back of his throat. "I did. He was from the museum in Dublin, from the Clan O'Leary." He looked up at the ceiling, his corded throat struggled to swallow. "They will, for the right reasons, use dark magic...

The vampires must have got to him before coming here."

Taking a moment to digest what that meant, her stark gaze lifted. The O'Learys aligned with the Morrigan. Jess had met two of their coven members a few years back. She couldn't imagine they would take the loss of one of their own easily.

"And they were prepared to use dark magic to protect the chalice..." The whispered words left her lips. "Where is it now?"

At the curt shake of his head, Jess raised her brows, shocked. "You won't tell me?"

Pacing away from her, he shoved his hands deep in his pockets. His raw fury buffered against her, as he turned, lifting beseeching eyes. "Jess, please. I *can't*. And we're all safer for it."

She watched Jason as he sat and stared back down at the floor, a lost expression in his eyes.

She fought her temper. "Now? You're waiting until now to start hiding things?" Whipping away from him, she stared out into the night.

Pressing her forehead against the cold glass, she closed her eyes, taking precious moments to face her anger head on, to not just let it control her.

She knew he would tell her if he could. Releasing a pent-up breath, she tried to keep the bite out of her voice. "Well, if you have all the answers, what about Seb, Jase? How do we help him?"

"Sebastian is an honorable man, and truth is very important to him. I know this."

Her reply backed-up in her throat, unspoken, as foolish, angry tears filled her vision, and Jason continued to speak. "He's not stupid—or selfish for that matter. He won't leave the museum. He just needs time. We can only hope he doesn't need too much."

She rubbed her temples to hide her burning eyes.

Searching to find a way to make this whole mess right, to think of a way to make him listen to her... Her voice scraped past the lump in her throat as she said, "At least now he knows we can find some way to cloak him."

Jase chuffed low in his throat. "Jess." Coming towards her, he wrapped her up in his big embrace. His awkward, brotherly patting on her head had her laughing through the tears and the sadness.

Pushing away from him, she looked into his stark gaze. "He got to me." She sniffed her way to the desk, pulling tissues from the box, mopping at her face. "He's got to me, dammit, and now I just want him here, till we can figure all this out, until I can make him listen to me, to tell him everything will be okay."

Heaving in short, weepy breaths, she slapped her palm on the desk. "Sodding-hell, I will not be some pathetic, miserable mess over a man."

Jason leaned back against the window, crossing his arms, a shadow of a smile racing across his face. "Too late for that, babe."

As she whirled on him, eyes flashing, he held his palms up in surrender. "Go see where he's at. The museum's a big place —and there's so much we still don't know about this whole poxy mess, it'd be better if we could all talk about it together."

Giving her a comforting smile, he softened his voice. "And maybe he'll listen to you."

Jess sat on the cold, flat, stone balustrade, looking down into the Reception Hall.

The glass display hanging from the ceiling threw shadows as the darkness surrounded her, interrupted by lights from outside. The whipping October winds raced over the terraces, and the heavy rain beat at the roof windows, echoing wildly.

The rain went unnoticed as she pushed from the balcony and dropped thirty feet to the floor.

The lights of the city flickered through the glass all around her.

She could feel all the visitors from earlier, could hear the soft hooves of the police horses a mile or more away, so alert were her senses.

But over all of those energies was his. She could feel his rage and savage confusion.

She was desperate to take to the air, to whip through the museum, jump into the winds and rush to him.

But he'd had enough to contend with for one day.

His scent was still thick against her skin, her body didn't feel like her own, and it was his fault.

His visage shimmered before her; the remembered heat of him as he'd held her, wrapped her around him, only a few hours ago. His lids had grown heavy and his body had hardened against her.

She cursed more useless tears and shook her head, this was not the time to discover her needy side. Focusing, she picked up his energy; his rage was pounding, she could feel it pulling her. He must be close.

She walked beneath the marble stairs, the darkness all encompassing. His scent carried the hint of sandstone, and rain.

But as she continued to walk, his rage spiked, filled with malice and violence. He'd found a vent for his anger.

She frowned into the night, seeking him, when the hot rush of his blood attacked her senses.

With a cry, she lifted her feet off the floor, and raced towards his energy.

Whipping her arms high, she pelted through the long corridor, towards the heavy doors. They were locked up tight, as she'd empowered them to be.

Electricity coursed around her system as she exploded towards him. Questions racing through her mind, while at the same time she was filled with a savage certainty that she was already too late.

The life-giving pulse of his blood drew her to him like a homing signal, but as she came upon him she struggled to comprehend what lay before her.

A writhing mass of dark figures.

Two lithe feminine forms wrapped around him; clearly visible was the long raven hair of one, and gold slave bands that encircled the honeyed skin of her upper arms. They glinted in the flickering light.

"No." The low moan dropped from her lips as she jerked to a halt, suspended, as everything clicked into place. The other three vampires had only been a diversion, so that these two could hide within the museum. They'd trapped themselves in here, inside her spell, and waited...

Seb's hand gripped the wrought iron balustrade, and in his other hand was a vicious double-edged knife that he must've pulled from one of the displays.

But they held him tightly. One had wrapped her legs around his middle as she undulated against him, her fangs at his neck freeing his blood so she could pull it from him.

The cropped-haired blonde held his head still as she fed from the other side. The blonde from the park...

Even with his shirt torn, his chest was barely discernible beneath the river of blood. The blonde had deep wounds to her arms and chest from his knife, her own blood running from her over him, over the punctures that littered his body.

"No. No. No, no, no." Jess barely registered her whispered litany, as she remained frozen, meters from the floor, in the shadow of the looming museum.

The panicked clap of her hands brought thunder, the deafening booms had them screeching and pulling free. The locked doors behind them clattered open on their hinges, slamming back against the sandstone walls of the Museum.

Two pairs of stunned eyes, swirling red and filled with lust, focused on her.

"Witch." The hissed whisper came from the tall blonde as she pushed up and away from his body. The darker of the two continued to straddle him, her wounds healing as Seb's blood coursed through her veins.

The blonde came quickly to her feet, licking a trail of blood from the soft skin of her inner wrist. "So good to see you again." Her husky words lilted with her strong accent.

With a slight smile at Jess, she tipped her head in elegant acknowledgment. "I hate to leave the safety of my hive. But this one, ah. He was worth coming out for—*très bon, non?*" Reaching down, she grasped the hand of her counterpart. "I will find the chalice. *Au revoir, chérie.*"

Jess raised sizzling balls of power in her palms, launching them. But it was too late, the air hazed around them, and they were gone.

She rushed to him, grabbing him by the belt of his jeans and under his arm, pulling him to her.

She could only just hear his heart pumping jerkily in his chest, his intermittent shallow breaths frightened her. Her options were few; he'd been bitten, their bloods had mixed. Jess had seen it with her own eyes.

Would he turn? Blood was a catalyst in magic and death, but was this the same?

Crouching over him, she placed her hand on his chest, his heart-beat weak, but constant.

As she knelt over him, the rain blew in, reaching her. The weather worsened with each minute, and the gusting wind carried his scent into the museum. His scent, which now carried the blood of a pack vampire. What should she do? There was only one person she could ask, and as her senses ramped up she knew that was no longer an option.

The sound of heavy footsteps grew louder as they echoed through the museum, then Jason's voice reverberated off the walls as he roared her name. The sound of Jason's footfall altered in a rush, heavily padded paws hit the marble as his unholy howl rent the air.

She was out of time.

Praying to the Goddess that she had the strength, she grabbed Seb's belt and as much of his shirt as she could, pulling him against her.

She drew every ounce of power she could harness, pulled it to her core and wrenched them both from the floor, as the sound of heavy claws, scrabbling for purchase, reached her.

Not daring to look back, she lifted them out, into the frigid night.

Hugging the shadows of the building she got them to a ledge, and wrapping him more securely around her, she lifted out, higher, into the dark, filthy weather.

The icy drops bit into her skin, as she weaved between the buildings, using every piece of cover she could find. Her mind raced. She couldn't go back to the hotel. Jason would track them in minutes. So could the female, if she was of a mind to.

She eased them down onto a dark rooftop. Propping him against the wet brick, she leant back against him, using her body to keep his upright, sharing her warmth.

She cast her eyes across the city. The Shard rose, glinting into the night sky, the dirty clouds shielding the very top.

She closed her eyes, searching through the melee of energy and weather static until she picked up what she was looking for. Keeping him at her back, she wrapped his arms around her shoulders, and gripping his forearms, she moved to the edge.

Conserving as much energy as she could, she moved across the rooftops, lifting them from one to another, until she reached her destination.

The azure blue water glowed, the endless pool was the crowning glory of this multi-million pound pad, which was thankfully sitting empty. From their place tucked in the shadows, she sent a well-aimed buzz of electricity, overloading the circuitry and shutting down the CCTV and pool lighting.

Hovering at the water's edge, she eased them in, shivering as the warm water surrounded her. Propping him up on the steps in the pool, he groaned low in his throat.

The sound startled her, and she held his face between her palms, whispering his name.

He seemed to calm at the sound of her voice, leaning into her.

The bolt of joy from him that hit her system left her buzzing. She hurriedly pulled him into the deeper water, knowing she'd need to use this energy-refill to get them out of the city.

She rolled him onto his back, sluicing water through his hair, rinsing the blood from both of them. It wouldn't free him from the vampire's mark, but water would make them harder to track—chlorinated water was even better. And she needed, desperately, to buy them some time.

Keeping his head on her shoulder, she gently embraced him, pulling his torso below the water. The feel of his hair-roughened chest wasn't lost on her, nor was the smooth skin as she ran her hands down his sides.

Slipping her fingers into his belt loops, she moved him through the gorgeously warming water.

His slick hair brushed against her neck, and as his body heated his scent rose, surrounding her.

She kept up her motion, but shut her eyes tight, raising her face to the sky.

He was unconscious, and she was lusting over him. Goddess, she needed help.

She walked them back towards the steps, softly talking to him. His heartbeat had grown stronger and more steady, but she had nothing to go on. Jess could only wait, and watch.

She had limited knowledge of vampires, only what she understood from Jason, and she had never heard of an attack like this. She hadn't even thought there were enough vampires left to fill a hive.

Her thoughts strayed to her family. She didn't have enough to go on to risk endangering them, and even if she did, Adam would most likely take the cull-first approach. That was if Jason didn't get to them first.

Her eyes glazed with hot tears of frustration at the possibility that he may just die, and she choked back a sob. Sitting down next to him on the step, she clutched his hand. The rain fell in a heavy deluge around them, and she wondered how long it would take for her to get them south.

"Jess." Her name sounded rough on his lips, and she lurched to kneel before him.

"Seb?"

His eyes were hazy with fever, but they were open and focused on her. "Where?"

Keeping her voice low, she shook her head. "Still in London. But we need to get out. Do you understand me?"

Sweat broke out on his forehead as he squinted at her. Fighting to concentrate, he gave a brief nod, his hand clenching and unclenching within hers. "My car?"

The mumbled words had her brows raising. Of course, he had a car, here in the city. "Do you have the keys?" She mentally kept everything crossed as he processed her words, and then he pitched forward, trying to move.

Catching his weight, she gasped, "Wait, wait. What do you need?"

"My pocket, check...pocket."

Holding her breath she couldn't believe it would be that easy. Feeling through the rough denim she made out the distinct outline of a fob key. Resting her forehead lightly against his, she let out a small laugh. "You're amazing. Where's it parked?"

He rubbed weakly at her hand, his breathing coming in rough pants, feverishly high color flagged his cheekbones, and all she wanted was to get him somewhere safe.

"Behind the hotel—near you. Street parking."

His words were so husky, as if it was taking great effort for him to form them.

Leaning into him, she lightly stroked his chest, as much to offer him comfort as to be sure that he was okay. "I'm going to get us there, you just have to trust me. Seb, did you hear me?"

His rough nod was her only answer, and she figured it would have to do. She backed up between his splayed thighs, taking his wrists she wrapped them around her shoulders and held on. Another shot of energy buzzed her system as he nuzzled against the side of her neck, and she consciously put her barriers up, figuring that his feelings would likely change as they left the ground.

Pushing away from the floor of the warm pool, she lifted them into the bitter night air. The rain was briefly abating, and she continued to whisper soft, meaningless words as they approached the edge of the rooftop.

The first building was relatively close, and she hoped he'd continue to lapse in and out of awareness as she moved them back towards the museum. Towards the hotel.

The towers that framed the entrance rose above the roofline of the Rembrandt to greet them, and she gladly made the last crossing, landing lightly on the hotel roof.

She looked down to the road below.

The North Terrace, turned onto Alexander Square, and she could see the nose of his Nissan from their viewpoint. She waited...waited to see if anything hit her senses, if anything felt off.

As they waited, he took more of his own weight. She didn't know whether to curse or cry. It would be so much easier to get him off this roof if he'd still been out of it.

Keeping his arm braced on her shoulder, she turned in his embrace to face him. He may be taking his own weight, but he was weaving on his feet, with shudders rippling across his chest and down his thighs.

"Seb, we're nearly there. Seb?"

The shudders intensified, as he huffed low in his throat. "Hear you, don't worry 'bout me."

Jess sunk her teeth into her lip as looked at him. "I need to get us off this roof. It'll be a bit of a...jerk, okay?" With her face pensive as she looked at him, she could only hope he had some idea of what was to come. "And when we get down there, we need to get in the car. Quickly."

She nodded encouragingly at him as she spoke.

His focus on her was intense; he was trying with everything he had to process her words. "Do trust you."

She knew that the watery smile she offered him was beaming, as she clenched his hands tightly in hers and drew him towards the lip of the roof. Sliding her hand into his pocket, she grabbed the key and hoped for the best.

Wrapping her arms around his waist, she clenched him to her, and stepped up onto the flat, stone cornice, drawing him with her. Rising to her tiptoes she placed her lips against his, and gripping the fob in her palm, stepped from the roof.

The wind rushed up to meet them, and she felt him go rigid in her embrace, as a shout left his lips.

She pressed the fob as they fell sixty feet towards the flagstone street.

Hearing the alarm disengage, she jerked them to a halt inches from the pavement. Seb crumpled in her embrace, and she tried, with as much gentleness as she could, to ease him to ground as she whirled and opened the door to the Pathfinder.

Jerking back, she grabbed him and, wrenching him to his feet, she all but dragged him, pushing and heaving to get him into the interior.

She had no idea if there was any danger, but she'd feel a hell of a lot safer once they were locked in.

Pushing him firmly inside, she slammed the door and raced to the driver's side, clambering into her seat.

Slamming her door, she clicked the central locking before turning the ignition. The engine roared to life on the silent street.

Reaching across him, she grabbed the seatbelt, strapping him in and then herself, and shoved the beast of a car into gear.

As they pulled onto the main road she fiddled about with the satnav, until finally managing to deactivate the GPS. She had no idea if they could be tracked, but she wasn't taking any chances.

She glanced furtively over at him. He looked to be sleeping. Peacefully relaxed—maybe he felt safe in his own car, she had no idea. But for now, she weaved in and out of the side roads. The orange street lights bouncing off the slick streets made her wince, as she crisscrossed London until they reached the A3.

The roads were empty in these wee small hours, and she did her best to avoid the street cams and speed traps, as they raced back to the bay, heading for home, where she was strongest.

Where they were safest.

CHAPTER 9

SHE STOOD in her lounge with Seb laid carefully at her feet, and breathed deeply, trying to replenish her lungs after virtually dragging him into the house.

Kneeling beside him, she closed her eyes and raised her palms. Taking a deep breath, she stilled, reaching out into the ether to seek her sister, and her brother.

She found Thea exactly where she was supposed to be; hours away in York. Adam was on his boat, by the feel of it. Probably nursing a large Scotch.

Remaining wholly still, she let the peace of the bay flood her, and reached out to the spirits that had been with her since she was a child.

> "Protect us from outside eyes
> See nothing, dim the lights
> Keep us safe tonight
> As I will it
> So mote it be"

Her words drifted up and hazed, as if filled with heat. She

felt the peace of confirmation settle within her. The spirits had come to her aid. They were safe. For now.

Reaching down to him, she felt his pulse and breathing were steady, and yet he still rolled in and out of consciousness, delirious ramblings falling from his lips. Unsure if she had the energy left to get him to the bed, she went to fetch blankets and pillows. Exhaustion pulled at her and she knew there was nothing left to do now, but let him fight the poisonous blood that roiled through him.

∼

HIS SKIN WAS HOT; burning. And his breaths came fast and heated against her.

She'd lain on the sofa to sleep, and at some point he'd clearly moved from the floor. He was wrapped around her, his body heat searing against her back, and the sudden tightening of his grip snapped her from sleep.

She gasped as fangs scraped her skin. He groaned against her, his moist tongue working her neck in soft laps, and she moaned in return, unable to move as shivers raced up her spine, curling behind her ears.

Each brush of his teeth had her nipples tightening, and she felt herself become wet in a rush. For a few short seconds, she whimpered in his grasp, until he became still, settling his lips as if to make a bite.

Gasping for breath, she wrenched away, coming to her senses. Pushing at him, she rolled, pulling them both from the sofa. They landed on the floor in a heap.

His eyes didn't open, he just rolled onto his back, and slept on. She lurched to her feet in a rush, dizzy from exhaustion.

"Oh, by the gods." Jess stared down at him, her hand touching her neck. It was still damp from his tongue.

She looked around, struggling to get her bearings.

Cuffs—she needed cuffs for just such an occasion.

She raced to her bedroom, feeling the pull of old power. She sat at the ornate wooden dresser and opened the center drawer. Phials of herbs, crystals and magical items lay before her.

Jess reached for the small wooden chest, a doorway to a stash of items that she could always access if she needed them...

Holding her palm above the open casket, she drew an image of the shackles to mind, before reaching in, and pulling them out.

She'd been so grateful to Thea for showing her how to set this up, it reminded her anew of how much she loved her crazy siblings—although this probably wasn't what Thea thought she'd be using a location spell for. Lurching from the dresser, she threw thanks to the spirits, making rash promises of endless mint humbugs.

The cuffs hummed with power, and kneeling beside him, she carefully locked the ornate shackles on each wrist, surprised by the urge to be gentle, considering how he'd just been about to bite her.

"Now, what do I do with you?" She rested her palm on her thigh and stared down at him, stroking his forearm.

As if in answer, his eyes flicked open, fastening on her. She jerked back in shock, before giving herself an internal shake. Dammit, she was also a creature of bitchass power, and she was not about to start jumping at shadows. "You're awake, then? Hungry, I suppose?" The sarcasm in her voice was lost on him as he frowned up at her in confusion.

"Jess?"

"Dammit, Seb." Her anger spiked, to protect her from the very real fear that she might've already lost him "Why didn't you warn me?!"

"You filled my dreams." His quietly spoken words floored her.

"You dreamed of me?" She found she had unknowingly clutched his hand, leaning closer to draw in his lush scent.

"I did. I dreamed of you in the rain, watching me. I dreamed..." His words died, as his eyes clouded then went wide. "NO! No." He sprang to his feet, the speed knocking her flat.

As he loomed over her, his eyes pooled black. He jerked confusedly at the shackles on his wrists, shaking his bound hands at her. "What is this? What?" He came down over her, straddling her thighs, much as the female had done to him hours earlier.

Stunned by the speed of his movements, she had no time before he came down on her hips, his jean-clad thighs trapping her against the floor, his bare chest covered in a sheen of sweat.

Keeping her hands flat against the carpet, she tried to stay calm and still, so as not to push his rage, not wanting him to lose control. "Seb, listen to me." She kept her voice slow and soft. "I *was* looking for you, and I did come for you, as soon as I knew something was wrong—"

"No! These...why these?" He shook the shackles at her, his eyes were dazed. Lost. "What happened?" His voice broke on the last, and his form crumpled over her; his chin touched his chest as a raw wounded sound reverberated through him.

Jess lay still beneath him, her elbows lifting her a little from the floor, as yet another wave of tears flooded her vision.

"Seb." Her breath caught on his name, as the tears tracked into her hair. "I can try and explain. I can be here with you." She came to an awkward sitting position, all thought of danger lost in the face of his pain. She pushed inside the loop of his cuffed wrists and wrapped her arms around his waist. "I can help... I can."

He rested his cheek against her hair, heaving in great breaths... Breathing?

"You're breathing?" She raised her face to look up at his, and watched with a mix of horror and anticipation as his eyes changed, filling completely with an inky blackness.

His arms tightened around her, pinning hers around his body. His lips parted, and she watched his fangs lengthen. She began to pant in reaction, the soft bruise at her neck burned and the shivery sensation returned. She had to fight the all-consuming need to drop back and offer herself up to him. What the hell was happening?

"Sebastian." She stayed rigid in his grasp, unable to sense anything other than his hunger, she struggled to keep her voice clear and precise. "Seb. I don't want to hurt you. But I will. You have to let me go." His head tilted to the side in confusion, and she knew she had no choice left. She could feel the metal of his cuffs digging into her spine, and cursed herself for being in this unbelievably stupid position.

Knowing this was going to sting like a bitch, she gritted her teeth and closed her eyes, feeling the charge emanating from her core she willed a pulse to the surface.

The electric jolt surged from her and stunned him. The veins corded in his throat as the current raced through his body, hitting the metal of the cuffs and re-entering her. She groaned at the pain, but still managed to shove him back and pull out from the loop of his arms, moving away in a rush.

The second the contact between them was broken, he was recovering, pushing to his feet and coming towards her.

She allowed him to back her across the room until she rested against the cool wooden door, where she raised her hands towards him; palms out, fingers splayed. "Seb, it's been a while since I've been tazed—and never by my own bolts—

which aggravates me no end. But believe me when I tell you, I will shoot you across this room if you don't stand down."

He came to a standstill before her, his eyes shimmering from brown to black. It was like watching a poltergeist possessing a new host.

Jess waited, watching him, keeping her hands charged to issue a bolt. She hoped that a couple of shots would be enough, extended use of energy like this drained her very quickly, and she had little left as it was.

Winging it here. Flash out of other options.

His cuffed hands hung in front of him and what was left of his shirt revealed the mess they had made of his chest. The wounds from the fangs that had pierced his body had closed, leaving marks in their wake, and her own bombarded senses wanted to touch him. Wanted to calm him.

Despite the danger, his change seemed to have amplified her reaction to him.

The emotion between them pulled at her, but now she was at a loss. Did this mean that he needed her only to feed?

Her heart clenched at the thought of all they'd missed out on. He'd been right; life really was too short not to just go for it.

"Jessica." His voice was mesmeric as he whispered her name. "Jess help me, I don't know... I need... I ache... What? What do I need, Jess?"

"I don't know." She yearned to ease him. "I think that your eyes changing is a sign that you need to feed—but you shouldn't be breathing. You—a turned vampire—are *a scourge*..." Repeating Jason's words filled her with sadness as she looked at Seb. They had gone from friends to enemies in mere moments.

"A vampire. Me?"

"What do you remember, Seb?" She reached out gently and took his hands, using his exhausted confusion to steer him, leading him back to the dim lounge. "Come, sit with me. We'll work it through from when you left——"

"Jason! I hadn't even thought. Will he... Can he do anything?"

The sudden look of relief on his face nearly broke her, and as she slowly shook her head she watched his hope race away like autumn leaves in the breeze. "No." She bowed her head, her own sadness at the loss of her best friend nearly flooring her. She'd drawn a line and chosen her side. Her loyalty had been tested...

"There is nothing he can do now, nothing anyone can do. It's more than rules, it's ingrained in him. You're a vampire and he's..."

~

SEB WATCHED her search for the words, distracted by her teeth capturing her bottom lip as she struggled with an explanation.

He wanted to lick where her teeth had been. Her words were hard to decipher over the silky tone of her voice as it rubbed across his skin, and the heavy weight of his sack in his jeans was a stark reminder that even though everything had gone to hell, his shaft still remained hard—for her.

She'd been in his dreams, her skin close to his, soft and warm. The taste of her sat on the back of his tongue. Her hands had felt soft on his skin, the water warm around them. Water?

"Seb?"

He snapped his gaze back to hers, feeling that same mindless need to have her—the closer she got the worse it became.

"Seb!" She pushed away from him, rising to her feet, static crackling in her palms as she held them up at him. "When that happens you're going to have to try and warn me. You can't just tune out and think that you'll be tapping me up for a snack. I am not, nor have I ever been, a *food source*."

He came to his feet, towering over her. He could feel her power, scent her skin, her hair...

"Food? What? Food is the last thing on my mind. I can feel you. I can smell you. I want to touch you. My skin is burning." He clenched his head, scraping his hands back through his hair.

His blood pounded through him, the beat of his heart reverberated like a bass drum. He stared at her, her long dark hair, pearlescent skin, the swell of her breast and curve of her hip. "I'm so tired, but when I close my eyes you're there; something is urging me to seize you, to touch you." His face came close and the heat of his breath and body nigh-on overwhelmed her. The way he drew her scent into him was like a physical pull.

His lashes lifted to reveal the swirling interchangeable depths of his eyes. "I need to taste you."

∾

THE POWER in her palms faded away as her body softened at his words. Desire coursed through her and she was too tired to think. She just didn't want to fight it.

She'd expected a rage of hunger, violent and uncontrollable, but his lips cushioned against hers.

His breath was ragged, in direct opposite to the gentle pressure of his mouth.

Easing her lips apart, the sweep of his tongue and scrape of teeth and fangs made her catch her breath, passion and a hint of fear rolling together in a heady mix. It had been so long, it seemed so long since she'd been held against him—there had never been another like him.

He gripped her wrists between them, holding her against the door, using his body to cage her in.

The strong heavy beat of his heart matched her own, and his muscles flexed as he leant against her.

Her mind fought to regain control, while her body heated and readied for him. Never had she felt such a need to touch a man's skin. Lifting her hands within his grasp she splayed her fingers, loving the feel of corded muscle beneath her palms.

He stilled, slowly drawing his head back a fraction. His black eyes focused on her face, her eyes, her lips, studying her, before leaning forward. He touched his tongue to her bottom lip, mouthing across her jaw before offering the tip of his tongue to the delicate skin behind her ear.

This time, she arched her neck without thought.

His lips were hot against the skin at her hairline, while his stubbled jaw scraped her neck. The heat of his breath forced her skin to shiver as his cuffed hands embraced her jaw, the chain linking them together resting low against her throat.

His fingers teased into her hair. She knew he was angling her for better access to her neck, and she felt a confusing compulsion to urge him on, instead of what should be a natural urge to fight him off; she relaxed in his grasp, releasing a whimper as she pushed up and against him.

His lengthened fangs trailed over her skin, and she could stand it no longer.

Grasping handfuls of his hair, her nails scraped his scalp pulling him closer, as she turned her jaw to offer him better access.

He waited, suspended for a moment in time, each panted breath a promise against her skin, before placing his fangs against her.

His long, heavy moan reverberated through her. But as her nails grazed his neck, he pulled back from her fingertips, the warmth of his body and pressure of his weight gone as he yanked away, backing across the room, stumbling to his knees on the carpeted floor.

He pulled in heaving, ragged breaths, his eyes clenched shut as his body shook.

Fisting his hands on the carpet, his head dropped forward. His dark hair hung into his eyes and the mass of chest and shoulder that was visible through the tattered shirt glistened.

She clenched her thighs involuntarily against the ache, stunning herself by calculating how hard it would be to wrestle him from his jeans, all the while wondering what the hell she was playing at.

He was a *vampire*. She should not be encouraging him to bite her!

≈

"WHAT THE HELL WERE YOU DOING?"

His coarse words had her frowning. "Me?" She spread her palms in question before sliding her gaze guiltily away on a mutter. "I'd have thought that was obvious."

"Obvious? Christ, Jess, I'm sorry—I was going to bite you! And then you weren't there anymore. Then it was her, and—"

"Her? Are you kidding me? I offer...and you're thinking of someone else?!"

He watched as her hair undulated away from her body as her temper rose, her eyes eclipsed, glowing lavender, the mesmeric swirl drawing him in. Her fists and eyes clenched, as she breathed heavily, her feet leaving the floor.

Coming to his knees, exhaustion swept through him in a rush, Jess was *levitating* and he was a *vampire*. His head fell forward, and he rapidly blinked, bewildered. "Jess, what's happening?"

～

FOR THE SECOND time that hour she found herself torn between his pain and her anger.

What had happened to her? Her usual humor and sense of what-will-be had been broken, by him. A man. Now a vampire.

Her booted feet hit the floor with a bump, and she took a shuddering step back as her mind tried to process how quickly this had become so screwed up.

Jess felt the chill fall through her as she stared down at him, and he stared up at her, his eyes confused, his hands cuffed and his body covered in bites.

What had she been thinking?

"Jess?"

The creature within him waged a war that was clearly visible in his still interchanging eyes, and once again Jess questioned how his heart still beat and breath filled his lungs.

The pack vampire had bitten him, and he'd clearly turned. Surely, he should be enraged, fighting to return to his Sire? The thought of the female rewarding him crawled through her, and the image of her slim arms encased in slave bangles wrapped around him would be forever stamped in her memory.

"Jess, say something...anything!"

He rose before her, his scent rushed through her senses. *What was happening?* She let out a shuddering release of breath, and wished for a scrap of control over her own body —just a moment to clearly focus.

She held her silence and willed herself to process a logical response. Logic was always her fail-safe; she needed to assess the situation to be able to move forward, and for that she needed information; as much as she could gather.

"Seb, step back. Space... I think we need space between us
—physical space. We need to think."

~

HE MOVED BACK, watching warily as her features set with
each step, her eyes cleared back to brown, revealing nothing.
His ability to read and judge the emotions and reactions of
others had always been strong, but now he could literally *feel*
her withdrawal.

The connection between them that had brought such
heat, chilled. Would this be the same with everyone? Would
he be able to detect base emotion—or was it just her? The
physical distance between them lifted a portion of the haze,
allowing him to focus his thoughts, and to process, for the
first time, the difference. To feel and hear the changes
within him.

~

SHE LOOKED at the four feet of distance they had put
between them, then at him as he stood framed by the
window, the sun encircling him. The sun?

She stared past him, out of the window, and he turned to
follow her gaze.

Do I know nothing about vampires? Never, before last night,
had she knowingly seen one.

Now she'd seen *six.* She'd killed two of them, and had one
in her living room, who stood at the window, as weak sunlight
reflected off and prismed across the walls and ceiling
around him.

For what seemed like the hundredth time in the last
twenty-four hours, she lifted her eyes skyward. *What the hell is
going on?*

"Jess, how am I standing in the sunlight?"

Her little voice was screaming long-practiced warnings to hold back, until she could figure out what was happening, while her gut was telling her to trust him.

She'd been keeping her magic a secret for a decade.

A decade of finely honed skills outweighed a newly awakened libido, didn't it?

"Why am I not bursting into flames?"

Good question. She shrugged, casting her hand out before her, as if she could pluck the answers from thin air. But she also didn't want him to panic either. "I don't know. Maybe different hives have different traits? The movies are just... movies. Throw in a cup of human fear, and you've got hundreds of myths and old wives tales." She struggled to remain completely passive, rapidly flicking through everything she could rationalize that might make sense.

Yet, as she returned his stare, his head nodded ever so briefly, and he folded his arms across his chest—he'd clearly made a decision. "And this...this between us. Why does it feel so much stronger now?"

Starting to pace, Jess watched him watching her as she roamed around her living room. "I'm not sure, exactly, but I have heard that physical attraction between people—people who are *other*—is stronger." *Heard? Reading gossip on the Facebook pages of the O'Leary girls, you mean. Nice one, Jess.*

Promising vile retribution if her little voice didn't shut-up, Jess longed for patience. Although she had to admit her little voice had a point; her family did such a good job of protecting themselves, that they all knew about their magic was what their Nana had told them growing up.

And there'd been a lot more fancy and a lot less fact in those stories.

"Have you ever experienced anything this strong before?"

He stood stock-still. She could see him processing everything around him. Taking it in, storing it.

"No. But then I've never...with someone who was..." Her words trailed off as she watched him. A predatory glint shadowed his gaze. The slight smile that touched his lips had a feral edge that made her heart pound in her ears and her breath falter.

"Good." His voice was low. As he turned away, he took a step closer to the window. "Do you think I'd be alright to go outside?"

Nerves rioted through her. "You're newly turned, it's trial and error—with a big margin for error." She looked pointedly at him. "I don't think it's a good idea just yet."

All she knew for sure was that the shackles she'd put on him were charmed, and any creature held by them wouldn't be able to go more than a few feet from their captor. A fact she wouldn't be revealing until she had this all figured out.

She couldn't risk that he'd do something stupid, like leave, not until they understood what was happening. The vampire blood in his veins was as clear as a GPS signal, a bounty on his head.

And Jason would hunt them forever.

Them. Somehow all *this* had changed things to *them*.

Thea's reading of the tea leaves came back to her again. Never could she have imagined standing on opposite sides to Jason. But she couldn't let him hurt Seb. Not only would he never forgive himself, neither would she.

So what was she supposed to do now—go on the run with a vampire of indeterminate species? And what about when he needed to feed...?

"Seb? Are you hungry?" Her voice cracked as she spoke. She knew this could take them to a bad place, but they had to know what they dealing with.

Scraping his hand back through his hair he leant back

against the windowsill, a baffled look on his face. "Hungry? Jess, I don't think this is the time to worry about food."

She waited a beat, holding his gaze, waiting for him to process what she'd meant.

His jaw slackened as realization hit. Something akin to horror flashed across his features. "No! Jess, I won't be doing that—not to anyone. I just..." His voice broke as the words died in his throat and, unable to stay away, she rushed to him.

Feeling his hand tremble in hers, and seeing his frame begin to shudder, she pulled him down, to sit on the floor.

His breaths came in heaving gasps, and beads of sweat sat on his forehead.

"Hey now." Cupping his jaw, his skin was burning hot, another confusion to add the list; she'd always assumed vampires would be cold to the touch. "Calm down. Seb, what's going on?"

He'd closed his eyes tight as he shook his head, as if to clear it. "When she..." He swallowed, struggling to form the words. "...when she bit me, I felt it."

Softly stroking his arm, Jess waited, unsure she was going to like what he was telling her.

"She wanted my fear, that's what they *need*." His unconsciously palmed the marks that littered his chest. "That's why the other one bit me too, but I was so fucking angry. At you... at Jason, that I wasn't afraid. It's not just the blood that feeds them, Jess, it's the fear. The horror of their victims."

As his chin touched his chest, shuddering breaths left his body, and she could barely hear his final words. "I'd rather die than become that."

Panic bloomed to life within her; she'd have to watch him. And they'd have to get some answers, because the cuffs wouldn't be coming off until they did. Until she could keep him safe. Not unless she could get him to accept a binding spell that would keep him near her, and to do that she'd have to tell him what the cuffs did...

She was going round in circles.

Maybe Jason was the only one would who could help, but as it was, she wasn't strong enough to face an enraged were-wolf; her magic needed time to recoup, and she didn't know how much time they had.

Still slowly stroking his check, his breathing had deep-ened while she'd been lost in her thoughts, but as she lifted her eyes the heat of his gaze had locked on the rise and fall of her breasts.

His speed was breath-taking as he grabbed her, pushing her flat onto the carpet, his cuffed wrists holding her hands above her head.

She knew something crazy was seriously affecting her judgment, but the heat of him was searing, and she was so tired of trying to fight the attraction between them.

He nuzzled her jaw, his whiskers scraping her skin as if he was rubbing her scent into his. The weight of his hips pressed heavily between her spread thighs, and she fought back a moan as he rolled against her.

The constant ache she felt from his nearness was only growing stronger, and the urge to wrap her legs around him was almost undeniable.

His head lifted, and he gazed at their wrists; his bound by her shackles, hers bound by his hands.

His chest, tanned and barely covered, was frustratingly out of reach, and she bit her lip as she watched his layered muscles shift beneath torn cotton as he let go of her wrists and laced their fingers together.

Could she do this? Could she take what was on offer? Slake her lust with him?

She had no idea how this would end, but she'd chosen her

path, couldn't she at least enjoy all of him, while there was still time?

Bloody right I can.

He clearly wasn't going to hurt her, or anyone for that matter, and she was so tired of not being near him. She'd nearly lost him...

"Seb, you're filthy." She looked down at his tattered shirt and further, down the length of his jeans. She swept her eyes closed as heat and longing filled her face, and arched her hips to his.

With her voice barely a whisper, she said, "Wouldn't you like a shower?"

His eyes pooled black as he watched her, the soft rise and fall of her breasts against his chest seemed to mesmerize him.

"A shower?" The dazed tone of his voice pleased her, she wanted to keep him off balance, to stop him thinking about anything else, to enjoy this like it could actually be real.

CHAPTER 10

"Jess? You want me to take a shower? Heaven help me, I can't think straight."

Her smile had a wicked edge as she looked at him. "Heaven can't help us, Seb, and I'm tired of thinking." She eased her wrists from his grasp, looping them around his neck, taking a soft teasing kiss from his lips.

The gentle scent of honeysuckle surrounded him as her fingers teased the hair at the nape of his neck, making him shiver. Any hope he had of rational thought fled as she lifted her hips, the warm heat of her pressed against his shaft, and he groaned low in his throat.

Her soft palms came to rest on his chest, as she pushed out from under him, rising.

She took his hand in both of hers, tugging him to his feet, as she backed away, pulling him with her.

The darkness of the hallway leant her lavender irises an unearthly glow, and the thought struck him that he would follow those eyes anywhere, into any hell.

His mind whispered nonsensical words; words that went

unnoticed when faced with Jess, and the silky warmth of her hands enclosing his.

He felt no desire to fight the hypnotic pull he felt for her. Since he'd woken, the rage, panic and confusion had welled up, continually threatening a spiral of despair and madness. Only her closeness blocked it out, burned all thoughts from his mind, leaving nothing but the heavy weight of his sack, the rigid shaft that he was desperate to slide into her.

Images flickered through his mind of gripping her hips, palming her soft skin while her violet eyes watched.

Enough.

Jerking her to a stop a few inches from the door, he looped his cuffed wrists over her head, traveling the length of her body, gripping the cheeks of her buttocks.

Lifting her from the floor, he crushed her between his body and the wall, cupping her, grinding his hips against her softness to show her how badly he ached.

Her hands braced against his chest, as she lifted briefly startled eyes to his face, before they drifted shut.

He went still as he watched her; the flush on her cheekbones, her full lips slightly parted. Finally bringing his lips a breath away from hers, he pressed heavily against her, reveling in the undulations of her hips.

But it wasn't enough, he had to see her.

"Open your eyes."

~

OPENING HER EYES, she stared up into his. They were black, but now a lighter ring circled his irises, glowing. That same feral smile greeted her as she looked at him.

Circling his hips, he forced his shaft across the seam of her jeans, the heavy ridge pressing too briefly against the perfect spot, causing her ass to jerk in his grip in a desperate attempt to get closer.

But he had thoroughly wedged her in, his breath hot as he gazed at her. She felt the unfamiliar squirm of embarrassment; he was turning her on, watching her while he did. She'd never felt so exposed. He was learning her, and she was losing the upper hand...

Another slow roll of his hips and thoughts of keeping her wits about her were lost.

Clutching his shoulders, she wrapped her legs around his lean hips, linking her ankles together as her head tipped back against the wall, eyes closing on a sigh as she brought him that fraction closer to the empty, aching heart of her.

"Uh-uh, look at me."

The low whisper of his words sent a shiver across her skin, but the rolling of his hips had stopped, and she couldn't bear that.

He laid his lips on the skin just below her ear, and sucked hard enough to leave a slight mark, resuming the roll of his hips as he caught her gaze.

"If you don't look at me, how do I know if you like it?"

Her hips ached to thrust up, but she was trapped by the wall and his weight, and she was becoming increasingly frustrated by his *game*. She released a pent up breath, her voice scratchy as it came out. "Seb, I do. But I want..." Her voice trailed off.

"What do you want, Jess?"

She frowned as he continued to smile down at her.

"I..." She unclasped her legs, and he eased back a fraction of an inch to allow her feet to touch the floor, before softly saying, "I want these clothes off."

He gave her ass another heavy squeeze, as if in reward. "Okay."

Gripping the tattered fabric of his shirt, she began pushing it over his shoulders, she'd worry about the cuffs when she got to them—but before she could, he released her, lifting his arms over her head, stepping back to lean against the opposite wall, facing her.

"You first."

The dare in his voice was unmistakable, and the flip-flop in her stomach had her wondering if she was nervous or excited.

"Afraid?"

She baulked at his comment, as he threw her own word back at her. Glaring at him in the dimness, her eyes flickered as if electrified. She dropped her voice to a purr as she swept her hair over her shoulder. "Oh bless. Newly-turned halfling, you have no idea what it would take to scare me." She unzipped her boots, kicking them off, hoping he never discovered her irrational fear of frogs, before reaching for the hem of her t-shirt, yanking it up. His light tut had her stopping to stare at him, her shirt halted across her midriff.

"Slowly, Jess." Pushing away from the wall, his cuffed hands brushed hers as they both grasped the t-shirt. "It's not a race."

What little advantage the heel of her boots had given her was lost as he towered above her.

He gathered the cotton in his hands, leaning in to brush her lips with his, following with a slow delve of his tongue between her teeth, stroking her.

He felt the cotton give and stretch beneath his grip, and careful to avoid the swell of her breasts, he eased it over head, dragging the shirt up her arms and stopped.

Looping the shirt double, he secured her wrists, trapping her arms in front of her.

Her lush breasts were forced closer by the confinement of her arms, nearly spilling from the frothy black bra.

Her hair shimmered around her, her lavender eyes swirled with intensity as she looked up. She was breath-taking to him.

"Something tells me you don't have any intention of taking my cuffs off, so at least this way we're even."

Undoing her belt and the buttons of her jeans he knelt, tugging them down the smooth expanse of her legs, leaving her in sinfully small underwear. The tiny piece of lace was held in place by thin scraps of silk that crisscrossed over her hips. His breath shallowed as he traced the pattern it made on her skin.

Forcing himself not to rush, he leant forward, touching his tongue to her navel, before trailing licks and kisses up the center of her body.

His hands pressed flat, fanning across her stomach, soaking up the honeysuckle scent that was purely hers.

Her pearly skin was rose petal soft beneath his lips, and her little pants made his stomach clench.

The slender shape of her felt delicate, almost fragile, beneath the rough heat of his palms; the smooth slope of her stomach had him groaning. As he turned his face against her flesh, she trembled beneath him, and his fingers teased the underside of her bra.

Her bound hands settled on the back of his head, the coolness of her touch a welcome relief from the burning.

Looking up, her eyes glowed down at him. Her hair fell in waves around them, whispering across his forearms. The lush swell of her breasts were a breath away, and he couldn't wait any longer to feel the weight of her.

Coming to his feet, he trapped her bound hands between the press of their bodies. Reaching out, he traced the edge of her dainty bra, watching his darkly tanned skin touch her pale flesh.

Molding his palms around her, he finally held the lushness

of her breasts, loving the sound of her gasp as his thumbs swept over the tight nipples.

His gut clenched at the sound, and he allowed himself one more sweep of his thumbs before capturing her soft lips, taking kisses across her jaw. Easing his body away from hers, he whispered at her ear, "Help me get my clothes off, Jess."

Her heavy-lidded eyes looked down at his cuffs. As her eyes travelled up his body, it was as if he could feel her gaze. She took the tattered collar of his shirt in her hands, and caught his eyes. "Trust me?"

Offering her a single nod, her palms began to hum, crackling with electric. The blue fissions left her fingers, leaching into the fabric, turning it to dust across his body, leaving static in its wake.

Her little grin was alive with a mix of lust and mischief as she placed her palms together, letting the current travel through her, and the binding at her wrists dropped to the floor.

Reaching up to sweep her hair across her shoulder, she ran her finger down the center of his chest. "I can't be held for long."

Taking his hand, she pulled him into her hazy bedroom. The delicate line of her spine drew his eye to the sway of her hips, and the way the string sat between her round cheeks left him panting.

Her ass was perfect; neat and pert. His palms itched to touch and mold.

She flipped a switch, casting a low glow across the en suite, and turned on the shower. Letting the steam build and swirl around them.

There was so much of her to look at he didn't know where to begin as she came towards him.

Her waist nipped, to flair over full hips. Tiny strips of

black lace crossed her milky skin, and her long hair streamed across her shoulder, almost reaching her navel. Her lavender eyes radiated power, and he knew he was lost.

She looked like sin, and he needed to touch her.

Seb toed off his shoes as she came to a standstill before him. Her movements slow and deliberate as she grasped his belt, releasing the buckle, and then each button on his jeans.

Sliding her palms beneath the waistband across his hips, she pushed the denim, and boxers down his legs, her nails lightly scraping the top of his thighs as she did so.

Her eyes fastened on his cock, her tongue dabbing her lip as she looked at it, and he knew he stood a little prouder at the way her eyes had widened at the sight of him.

Taking a step away from him, her glance was almost coy as she reached behind her, releasing the clasp on her bra.

She shimmied the straps down her arms, and her beautiful breasts swayed with the rhythm, the dusky nipples already hard, waiting for his lips.

As she pushed the thong over her hips, she'd just dropped them to the floor when he moved, unable to wait a moment longer.

Taking her wrist, he pulled her to him, and his lips crashed onto hers, her arms wrapping around him.

He backed her into the shower, her gasp filling the air as he pressed her to the cold tiled wall, his kiss carnal and raw.

The hot water hit his back, sluicing down his skin, as he pressed against her. The mounds of her breasts pressed into his chest, her silky legs rubbed against his hair-roughened thighs.

Blood pounded around his body, roaring in his ears at his need to take her, and he broke their kiss. Licking a trail of water from her throat, groaning, as he tried desperately to claw back some control.

He wanted her to need him; wanted her to ache.

Taking a breath, he watched her heavy eyes open, watched her soft lips form his name as a question, as he went onto his knees before her.

Sliding his palms down the length of her thigh to her knee, he lifted her leg, slowly placing it over his shoulder, loving the excitement that flared in her eyes as he held her gaze.

"Don't move." He whispered the demand as he leant closer to her, keeping his eyes locked with hers as his tongue touched the smooth flesh of her pussy.

Her folds were slick, and he moaned against her, long and low as he delighted in her taste.

Her breaths were already coming fast, her small whimpers urging him on, as shivers raced through her.

He took slow laps, loving the way her legs trembled against him, as he settled into a slow circular rhythm, around the nub of her desire.

Her fingers clenched in his hair, bordering pain as she rolled her hips with him, following his tongue. And he loved it—the taste of her, the sounds of her panting cries and begging whispers, the movement of her body.

He kept up the soft motion of his tongue, as he trailed his fingertips up and down the inside of her thighs, drawing ever closer to the throbbing heat of her.

He heard the moment her cries changed, becoming almost desperate as she neared, and as much as it pained him, he drew away, leaving her on the cusp, her longing sighs ringing in his ears.

Standing up, he lifted his cuffed arms over her head, jerking her to him, picking her up.

The length of him slipped against her wet folds, making them both moan, until finally he pressed the head of his shaft to her center, pushing into her delicious tightness.

She fluttered around him, showing him how close she was, and he had to grit his teeth to stop from shoving into her slick depths.

But as her legs wrapped around his hips, he knew it was hopeless; the first sweet circling of her hips on him rent his control, sending him over the edge.

Pinning her back to the wall, he grasped her buttocks in his hands, kneading the flesh as he stroked fully into her.

Steam billowed around them as he made long surging thrusts into her sweet depths, the urge to come rolling up his back, as, finally, she broke around him, her high cry lifting.

He gritted his teeth, as her sheath clenched and she arched into him, urging him deeper.

Her feathery moans filled the shower stall, her head arched back in abandon as he watched her. A flush filled her face, her lips trembling as she came.

As her climax ebbed, he couldn't hold on any longer. But as he pulled from her, her hand instantly reached for his length.

Her grip was firm as she held him, and her moan rang out in unison with his at her first long, stroke.

The wet heat of her lips touched his jaw, as she leant into him. Her slippery breasts slid against his chest as she whispered to him, her words intensifying the pounding of his blood.

The heavy stroking of his shaft continued as the water sluiced across them.

He slitted his eyes open, finding her iridescent, glowing gaze watching him. Waiting for him to come.

With a shout he threw back his head, pumping into the watery jets, his lips finding hers and taking them, in a raw mating as she melted against him.

~

As his forehead touched hers, a satisfied smile touched her lips, and her eyes blinked slowly open, to be greeted by the sight of fangs.

Her breath caught, and, despite just having had a pretty spectacular orgasm, lust pooled at the sight of his sharp, pearly points. Who knew she had a dangerous complex?

His own eyes sleepily opened, water spiking his lashes, and as he smiled down at her, his normal brown eyes were now fully black, with the lighter ring from before seeping into the inky depths.

His lips gently meet hers, and his arms tightened warmly around her.

As she watched him, she realized he had no idea. His own satisfaction was clear in the long 'hmm' he murmured in her ear, as he rubbed himself against her, softly stroking her ass.

He seemed to be praising her?

Slowly pulling her away from the wall, he lifted his arms from around her, softly touching her face as he drew away, leaving her feeling suddenly bereft, even in the hot shower.

"Jess, can we take these cuffs off now?" Her eyes darted up at his question, and the alarm in her gaze brought him to a standstill. "What's the matter?"

She gestured towards him with a guilty shrug, not wanting to kill the mood. And even though she thought his fangs were hot, she needed to assess whether or not he had *other* urges building. "Your eyes, and your fangs... They're out."

As his tongue touched the tip of a lethally sharp fang she almost couldn't suppress the urge to moan. *What the hell is wrong with me?* "Do you feel anything? Rage, hunger... Anything at all?"

Pushing out of the shower, he wiped his big hand across the mirror, staring at himself.

She felt the tension begin a heavy churn through him, filling the room, and she mentally threw up her barriers.

She'd need to hoard the energetic boost their shower time had given her. If she was even remotely considering asking for Jason's help, she'd need enough juice to be able to hold off a crazy werewolf, and bloody good spell to hold him if he lost it...

Stepping from the shower, she caught his gaze in the mirror, and cautiously touched his shoulder. "Seb?"

Whirling on her, he threw his cuffed hands towards her. "Christ, Jess, you look like I'm about to attack you. I'm not a monster about to pounce! At least you sure didn't think so ten minutes ago."

Standing naked in front of an angry vampire didn't work for her, and she reached for a towel and wrapped it round herself. "That wasn't what I meant. I just thought you might be struggling against an urge, or something."

Clearly trying to hold on to his temper, he pulled a towel from the rack, struggling to wrap it round his hips until she helped him.

"This Jess," he gestured at the towel, "this is exactly it. I can't stay handcuffed until we can figure this out. I haven't hurt you, and the only *urge* I have is to take you back to bed. How dangerous can I be?"

"I don't want you to hurt yourself!" The words rushed from her lips as she jabbed him in the chest. "You said you'd rather *die* than feed, and that doesn't work for *me*." She stalked from the bathroom, slightly surprised to find October sunlight streaming into the bedroom.

Realization dawned as she stood in the middle of the room, dazedly turning full circle, rushing back to stop him from entering, only to find him a pace behind her, his face angry as he spoke.

"You honestly think I would kill myself?" He lifted his hands as he spoke, his tone incredulous. He sat on the edge of her bed, leaning his forearms on his spread legs, as he looked at her. "Let's not write me off just yet, Jess, okay?"

Rubbing her forehead at the start of a pounding headache she stared at him until he raised his brows at her. "What?" His tone was that of a belligerent teenager.

Furiously pointing at the window, she widened her eyes at him in exasperation. "Err... sunshine, bright, middle of the day sunshine."

Looking down at the midday rays that lay across his bare skin, he heaved in a sigh, his face mirroring the confusion she felt.

"Well, it didn't get me this morning, why would it now? What are we supposed to make of any of this?"

"I don't know." Huffing, she crossed the room, and sank down on the bed next to him, linking her hand with his. "I just wondered if the faint early morning light was too weak to count. Now, I don't know; maybe it's because we're inside, maybe it has to be direct sunlight—I just don't know."

Pursing his lips he squeezed her hand. "Let's find out."

"What? Why?"

"Jess, we can't just sit here and wait to see if I suddenly become some rabid thing that you have to put-down. So let's get the answers while we can."

It was odd, having a man in her house. She'd found a hoodie of Adam's in the bedroom he'd stayed in, and thrown Seb's jeans in the dryer.

And here he was, getting dressed in her room, while she did, using her hairbrush, and standing at her mirror.

She laced up her walking boots, thinking all this 'getting dressed for the day' business could be a big waste of time if his skin started to fry the minute they opened the door.

But he was *right*, they had to find out what they could, and the sooner the better. And despite their bitter overexposure to the elements as they'd raced out of London yesterday, the bright, crisp October afternoon was calling her.

Following him out into the living room, she stood at the patio doors. "Just stand back in the shadow, okay? Let me open the door, then edge forward, maybe put your hand out."

She could've slapped him for the amused look on his face, but she threw him a glare instead, and turned the key.

Easing the door open, the sharp sea air blew in, filling her lungs with home, and she clung to the desperate hope that everything was going to be okay. That they could get through this.

Slamming a lid on that thought, she looked back at him. She was going to have to deal with whatever it was between them, she knew that. She just wasn't ready to do it yet. And she had enough to *deal with* right now anyway.

Ignoring the faint cackling of the spirits that gently reached her, she mentally threatened a withdrawal of all mint humbugs, and it subsided into whispering titters.

His eyes had closed as the breeze reached him; he too seemed to be drawing strength from the salty wind. Slowly lifting his hand into the shaft of natural light, they both waited, breaths suspended.

Until her patience ran out. "Well?"

Looking up at her, wonder lit his face. "I can feel it."

Going to him, she slowly touched the back of his hand, shaking her head in question. "Feel what?"

Taking a step fully into the light, he walked towards the open door, his warm hand held hers, as he pulled her with him.

She was nervously watching him as they stepped outside, until he stopped suddenly, leaving her gasping and trying to pull him back indoors.

He was immovable. Racing round in front of him, the pure joy on his face tugged at her heart. "Seb?"

"I can *feel* the sea, Jess." He stared out over the dunes, looking at the rise and fall of the sandy knolls, and the yellow grasses that had always brought her such happiness, such peace.

"I can feel the salt on my skin, and the wind. I can smell *everything*."

She swallowed over the lump in her throat at the relief and happiness pouring from him. Reacting on instinct, she reached into her pocket and took out a key.

Taking his cuffed hands, she lifted wet eyes to him with a smile as she unclicked the lock. "We're going to work this out, okay?"

Undoing the cuffs, she pushed them in her pocket.

His warm palm slid along her jaw, lifting her face to his, so he could touch his lips to hers. The sweet bolt of happiness tripped through her like a lightning strike. Knowing her eyes would be glowing lavender, she looked up to find his own brown eyes, churning with a grey black mix, smiling into hers.

"Let's go down to the sea." Tugging her with him, he stepped off the decking onto the sand and pebbles, drawn as ever, to the water.

Jess looked across the long stretch of dunes and beach. A few dog-walkers loitered in the distance, but none strayed this far down. The late autumn sun had chased away the clouds, leaving a high bright sky. The crisp air still held tiny tendrils of summer that clung to the breeze, but it wouldn't be long before winter frosts cloaked the landscape, leaving a grey and churning sea.

The tide had drifted out, and the low surf meandered up the shore. Her hand was warm, wrapped in his, and her eyes stung with emotion and relief, as the sea refilled not only her energy, but gave her joy and calmed her soul.

Last night was a lifetime ago, and standing here on the

beach could be nothing more than a stolen weekend from London. If she wiped her mind she could believe for a minute that they'd snuck off, and they could go back to their normal lives.

Just for a minute.

But they couldn't.

His life had been ripped apart, and she'd stood with him, giving her loyalty to a man she hardly knew.

He bent down to pick up a shell, turning to show her the intricate spiral, and as she touched its ocean-washed smoothness she looked up at him, seeing in his eyes the spark that had drawn her to him in the first place—kindness, laughter, a sense of integrity. There was something innate that drew her to him, and seeing him in danger had blown that wide open, leaving her unable to hide it. She'd fallen for him. She'd be afraid later, she'd panic about not wanting to be tied down later. She'd fallen for him. She'd be afraid later, she'd panic about not wanting to be tied down later. She'd worry that it was all too soon, and too quick, *later*.

But as she stared up at him, feeling the smooth shell beneath her fingers, and letting the magnitude of the last weeks pour through her, she knew all the fear and panic in the world wouldn't change how she felt.

Acknowledging her feelings had them swelling up inside her, static fissions dancing from her fingertips vibrating the shell in his palm. He laughed at the tiny shocks that danced across his skin, and the natural markings of the shell turned lavender, winding round the spiral, changed forever.

Closing his hand, he put the shell in the pocket of his jeans. "I'll keep it. It'll be my charm."

Going on her toes, she pressed trembling lips to his, the act all the more intense for her self-admission. "It will always bring you luck."

Deepening the kiss, he threaded his fingers into her hair, making her shiver. His fangs were nothing more than little points as she twirled her tongue with his.

His arms wound round her waist, tightening as he pulled her closer to him, as he nipped and tasted her.

Gently easing away from him, she just stared, unsure of what she'd say if she spoke.

As the wind picked up her hair, he reached up, tucking it behind her ear, and grinned. "Pretty thing you are."

Laughing at his unexpected compliment, she smiled back, wanting to draw his attention away from her, away from the emotion she was sure was plainly printed on her face. "Why, thank you. And what about my beach, that's pretty spectacular too, huh?"

Glancing behind her and then back up at her little cottage, he nodded. "It's gorgeous. No wonder you like coming home." And just that quickly the moment was gone, reality flooded back in. "Jess."

His voice cracked as his head dropped to hers and she cupped his face in her palms. She shouldn't have taken off the damn cuffs. He'd convince himself that doing something stupid would be better for everyone, or some such crap. Just as she opened her mouth to threaten fire and brimstone if he tried anything, he lifted his head, his churning eyes alert as he looked around them, stiffening in her arms.

Whatever it was, he'd picked up on it seconds before her, and she looked around them with wide eyes, shocked that she'd been so idiotic as to think this was a good idea.

She turned hurriedly, grabbing his hand, pulling him with her. They shouldn't be this far out in the open.

Picking up pace, they broke into a run, across the sand and up onto the decking. Ushering him in, she closed and locked the patio door behind her, turning to find Jason standing before them.

A stunned shriek left her lips as she swept Seb behind her, power flying from her palms, capturing Jason with a bolt, lifting him from the floor.

He hung suspended, unable to move.

"Jess?" Seb had come to stand beside her. "Jess, let him go." He was stoic next to her. He'd thrown his shoulders back, like he was going to *do the right thing.*

She shook her head vigorously at his hushed words. Her hair was shaking around her, as she continued to keep Jason pinned. "I can't. You don't understand, Seb." Tears stung her eyes as she looked at the face of her friend; his eyes beginning to change as he fought her hold on him. Fought the confinement. "He'll have no control..." Her voice hitched, as her mind raced through ways to get them out of here without having to hurt Jason. "Once he scents vampire—"

The strength of Jason's beast was already pushing against her, desperate to rise up and protect him from her. She could feel her hold on him weakening with each second. She kept the beam as gentle as she could, not wanting to hurt him. But at her words his arms, head and shoulders broke free, his eyes narrowing with ferocity.

"Vampire." He dragged his hands across his body, trying to physically push off her binding, as he bellowed at her. "Vampire!"

A sob caught in her chest, his burning anger sweeping over her. It was taking everything she had to hold him.

When he realized she wasn't going to answer he whipped his eyes to Sebastian. "Where is it, Seb?" His voice was a low growl, as he repeated the words.

Seb hung his head, his hand on his chest. His words were barely a whisper as they scratched from his lips. "It's me, Jase. It's me..."

Holding him got suddenly easier as he abruptly stilled,

staring at Sebastian, his movements wolf-like as he scented the air, leaning forward as best he could.

Jess's heart was pounding in her chest, fear tripping along her nerve endings as she waited for the eruption. Knowing she'd have to strike him down.

But none came.

Jason's head reared back, confusion furrowed his brow as he shook his head. "You're a... You're a..." His voice trailed away.

Lifting his head, Seb gave him a sad smile, saying what his friend could not. "A vampire."

Jason's eyes widened in shock, and as Jess watched she knew she was missing something.

"What? No—"

"Jase." Seb's hushed voice cut of his friend's denial. "Please, Jase, I know we're sworn enemies or something like that..." Seb floundered for the words. "But I need you to help me."

Jason angled his head to look at Jess, and she could see his eyes had completely shed their wolfy rage. "Jess, for gods' sakes, will you let me bloody down." She hesitated. He seemed to have total control, but if she released him and he changed, she'd never hold him off...

"I can't, Jase. I can't let you hurt him, I know he's a v—"

Stopping her words with a huff, he crossed his arms. "Vampire—yes, I know that's what you two both think. But he's not."

Seb's head snapped up, as he walked across the room.

Jess gasped, drawing Jason closer to her, yanking him across the room away from Sebastian. "Seb! Will you get back!"

Jason's arms jerked out to steady himself, and he glared at her. "Bloody hell, woman! Will you stop spinning me around? I'm liable to throw up."

Seb turned on Jess, raising his hands in exasperation. "Jess, will you please just put him down." Turning to Jason, he looked questioningly at his friend, his eyes full of hope. "Then what am I?"

A raw grin split Jason's handsome face. "Buddy, you're a wolf."

CHAPTER 11

"WHAT!" Jason hit the floor as Jess abruptly dropped her palms, her voice incredulous. "He's a what?"

Staying on the floor, Jason chuckled, staring at her, the chuckle leading into a full blown laugh. "You thought he was a *vampire.*" Pushing his hair away from his forehead, he whistled. "Man-oh-man, that's a good one. Clearly, I need to explain a few things to you guys about vampires."

Jess looked over at Seb, who seemed rooted to the spot, his hands on his hips as he frowned at Jason. "*I'm,*" he patted his chest as he spoke, "a wolf? Me?"

Jason raised his brows, gesturing at the window. "You don't think it's odd that you're standing here in the *daylight,* having just come back from a cozy walk on a *sunny* beach?"

Jess inwardly cringed. "Of course we did." Her tone waspish as she spoke. "But you and I have never hashed out the truth and myth of it all. You only have to *hear* the word vampire, and you're all raged up. So everything I know comes from the movies." Throwing her hands in the air, she turned away, muttering, "Maybe they can day-walk, for all I know. Wesley Snipes managed it."

Jason roared with laughter, pushing himself to his feet. Crossing to Sebastian, he stopped in front of him, looking at him, lifting his head, he tested his scent. "You're a wolf. No doubt about it." Wrapping him in a hug, he slapped his back.

Jess looked on as Seb slowly hugged him in return, laughing, his shoulders shaking as they broke apart.

"Oh, man." Bending over, Seb braced his hands on his thighs, heaving in a huge breath, the releasing sigh full of relief. Shaking his arms out at his sides, he rolled his shoulders, his slightly delirious laughter pulling a bewildered smile from her.

He turned shocked eyes to her, still shaking his head in wonder. "I'm not a vampire."

Still unable to process exactly what was happening, she gave him what she hoped was a positive nod. "Apparently not."

Jason shrugged, a slight frown creasing his forehead. "No, you're not. But I will tell you what you are." With a sharp point of his finger, he jabbed Seb in the chest. "You're a bloody liar. What *didn't* you tell me about what happened in Canada?"

As Seb opened his mouth to speak, Jason held up his hand, cutting him off. Moving to him, Jason walked round him, taking in his scent once more, his eyes wide. "Holy crap —before we get to that, I can smell your hunger. Have you eaten since you began the change?"

"No. I..." His voice trailed away as he nodded at Jess, lowering his voice. "I didn't wanna worry her."

Jason's look was one of horror. "Mate! You must be starving. A newly-turning wolf has needs."

At his groan of agreement, Jess released a huff, her own voice rising. "I asked if you were hungry! Why did you say no, Seb? I just—"

Their words layered across each other.

"Jess, I thought being hungry meant I'd have to feed...and you know I wouldn't..." He trailed off awkwardly as he looked between her and Jason.

Flipping her hair back from her face, she grimaced. "That's why I *asked*! We'd have worked something out." Throwing her hands in the air, and stopping them all, she took a settling breath. "But enough. If you're hungry, for gods' sakes, let's eat."

Walking into the kitchen, she went through the side door that led to the garage, opening her chest freezer. Knowing how greedy Jason's appetite could be after a change or a night run, she rummaged around, loading things onto a tray. Cooking wasn't her area, but she'd figure something out.

Laying them out in order of cooking time, she turned on the oven, sliding in a couple of pizzas.

"I know pizza is a pretty poor offering, but it'll cook quickly, and we'll work from there."

Jason had slid onto a stool next to Seb at the breakfast bar, pushing a carton of milk at his friend.

He looked quietly happy with himself. Every time she caught his gaze, he was nonchalantly grinning or throwing her a wink, until eventually she lost her ability to ignore him.

Rolling the pizza cutter through the bubbling cheese, she carried the plate over to them, dropping it onto the side with a thump. "Alright, go on. Laugh all you like. Yes, I thought he was a vampire. Crazy me."

Seb groaned at his first mouthful. "Food."

Grinning at Seb, Jason turned his amused gaze to her. "Oh, come on, Jess, you've got to admit, it's pretty funny. Sod the daylight, but the fact that he hadn't torn you limb from limb should've tipped you off."

The microwave pinged, having defrosted a stew that Thea had made, and Jess put the crockpot in the hot oven, and dropped half a dozen frozen rolls into the warming drawer below.

"Would I have done that? Would I have lost control of myself?" Seb's solemn question left Jason serious, chasing the laughter away as he faced his friend.

"Yes. You would have been driven by blood lust, controlled by an overpowering urge to hunt and kill. As a turned vampire, it's unlikely you would ever be able to control that urge. Which is why they don't turn humans." Taking a breath, Jason clasped his hands in front of him, visibly controlling the icy fury at just having to speak about them. "Vampires see all other creatures as nothing more than sport." Reaching for the milk, he poured himself a glass, and refilled Seb's empty one. "Except us. We are the only thing they actively fear."

Jess swallowed as both Jason and Seb's eyes glowed as they spoke, the lighter ring that had been creeping into Seb's gaze, now virtually eclipsed the black. It had the same intense blue hue as Jason's eyes when his beast woke.

Picking up his glass, Seb gave a curt nod. "Good. They should fear me." His words were low and deadly.

Desire burned through her as she watched him speak. She turned away, busying herself. It would seem she most definitely had a thing for danger. Rolling her eyes, she wondered what else she'd discover about herself as this little escapade continued.

As they continued to talk, she pulled out plates and set to preparing more food.

She was tending him, feeding him, making him happy, and it felt good. Strange but right. Not mundane...

Yes, because having two werewolves in your kitchen is so ordinary. Wondering if any sort of spell could shut out her little voice, she ignored it, blithely returning to her thoughts.

She'd never imagined herself playing the little woman, but

she'd been horrified at the thought of his hunger. She couldn't tolerate the thought of him being in danger...and she was desperate for him to bite her.

It was turning into an illuminating twenty-four hours.

"Now you've polished off the first wave of food, you can start talking before round two begins. What happened in Canada, Seb?"

Jason's question had her turning, leaning against the breakfast bar, facing them.

Seb dropped a crust to his plate, his gaze solemn as he looked between the two of them, his voice quiet. "I don't remember much."

Lacing his hands behind his head, Jason leant back against the wall. "I can't help you if you won't talk to me. And I know it was something more than *frost* that bit you."

Nodding jerkily, Seb pushed to his feet. "Oh, it bit me alright."

Standing before them, he dragged the hoodie over his head, dropping it on his chair, before unbuckling his jeans.

Despite her confusion, Jess felt her mouth dry at the glorious site of muscle and skin. She couldn't wrap her mind around what he was doing. She'd seen him naked, what had she missed?

Turning his back to them, he dragged the waistband lower over the left side of his hip.

Jess caught her breath as he revealed the viscous scar that marred the skin of his lower back.

Four large incisors had caused the most damage, tearing into him, leaving long deep rips.

Unaware of what she was doing, she walked to him, placing her right hand on his back. "Seb." As she whispered his name, she gently laid her left hand against the still healing scar tissue.

She felt him tense beneath her palm, and she unconsciously murmured praise as she touched his searingly hot skin.

Her stomach churned thinking about what he'd gone through; the creature must have been huge, the bite spread longer than the length of her hand. "You must have been so afraid. I wish I'd been there."

Turning to her, he cupped her jaw, placing a soft kiss on her lips. "Thank you, Baby, but I'm glad you weren't."

His eyes swirled, the black becoming bluer each time they changed, and she stayed locked within his gaze, until Jason's words broke the silence.

"Okay, then, so that answers more than one of my questions. But Jess, I gotta ask, when you guys were," he coughed into his palm and raised his brows at them, "you didn't think the scar was a little off?"

Turning angry eyes to explain that she'd been a little *busy* at the time, she opened her mouth to speak, when a rough growl rumbled from Seb.

As Jess looked up, his canines lengthened before her eyes, looking longer and more lethal than she'd ever seen them. "Sebastian?"

Rearing back, Seb put his hands up, backing away from them as his breathing deepened, his brows raised in shock. The blue had almost eclipsed his irises, leaving only a thin ring of black remaining. "Christ, I'm sorry, I don't know..."

Chuckling, Jason got up, heading for the oven, pulling out the crock-pot. "I wondered what would happen if I brought up Jess." Nodding towards her, he locked eyes with Seb. "You're going to have to learn to control that." Lifting the lid, he stirred the contents, letting the heady smells of meat and gravy fill the kitchen. "A wolf is always irrational when it comes to his mate."

"His *what?*" Jess was tired of sounding like an idiot. She was also sure she probably didn't want to know where this was headed. But it was too late now... "Jase, there's a lot that you're not telling us."

~

SETTING the bowl of warm rolls next to the stew, Jess came to sit down next to him, as Jason sat down across the table.

Jase pointed at the stew. "You eat. You need it. And I'll talk...and eat. I'm hungry."

Ladling the delicious food into his bowl Seb looked at Jason, waiting for him to begin.

"You're going to have to tell me if you feel angry, or if you feel like you're going to lose it. Some of this *discussion* is going to involve Jess, and your wolf isn't going to like me talking about her in *that* way. It'd be easier on you if she wasn't here, but it's important that you both know what you're dealing with. So, it is what it is."

Listening to the nervous edge in Jason's voice, trepidation trickled through Seb. The rage had risen from nowhere, and it had been sharp and instant. The only thing that had stopped him lunging for Jason before had been the fact that Jess stood between them.

As if reading his thoughts, she laid her palm across his thigh, softly rubbing, easing his tension. "I'll try. But if it was like just now, I didn't even see it coming."

"It won't happen like that once you've made your first change. You'll have more time to get control, but rage and lust are the two biggest problems we battle."

Jess's spoon halted halfway to her lips, and he gritted his teeth at her discomfort.

"Why haven't I changed yet? It's been months since I was bitten."

"Just being bitten isn't enough to turn you. As a human, you should've just remained dormant. But you've encountered a catalyst, something that set off the rage of your beast, and he is driven by the need to protect you. You *and* your mate."

Jason kept his eyes locked solely on Seb's as he spoke, but he could feel Jess squirm beside him. He tried to ignore the trickle of doubt that touched his conscious. What if she didn't want to be his mate?

The force inside him roiled at the thought, and it took all his control not to drag her away, back to bed, and sate her until she had no other thoughts but him.

"Being bitten by the vampires was the catalyst?" His words were gravelly when he spoke, and Jason held up his palms, deliberately leaning away from the table, opening his body language.

Seb could feel his body temperature rising, the heavy weight in gut beginning to prowl. But as he fought for control, Jess slid her cool, soft hand into his. Her calm smile relaxed, what he was now realizing, was his beast. Her soft words and gentle touch settled the creature, soothed him. "It's alright."

Nodding, he took another mouthful of the stew, breathing in deeply as he chewed. The rhythm of the action calming him further. He nodded at Jason to continue.

"I would say that being bitten certainly had a part to play. But it could have been a number of factors. I'm going to need to talk about Jess now, alright?"

Pushing the bowl away, Seb leant back in his chair, taking her hand between his.

Lacing his fingers with hers, he smoothed the soft skin on the inside of her wrist, liking the way her pulse jumped.

Nodding, Seb searched for the right words. "Okay. Just— just try not to be too..." Finally, he just shrugged. "I'll tell you when there's trouble."

"Sure thing, buddy." Pushing his own empty bowl away, Jason loosely clasped his hands on the table. "It could be that

Jess has triggered your wolf; her leaving for Greece, or her coming back?" Leaning back in the chair he gazed into the distance, clearly trying to organize his thoughts.

"That night in the Hospital, I knew you'd had a run-in with something. But you said it was a few bruises." Jason arched a brow in his direction, and Seb merely shrugged it off. "So I didn't push further, and today is the first time I can tell your scent has changed from human to wolf..."

Jason glanced towards the window, his voice softening when he said, "Your wolf clearly recognizes Jess as your mate, and if you weren't already sleeping together when the vampires attacked, it's more than likely that your wolf rose up to protect her. And then to *claim* her."

Even though Jason had kept his references to Jess as respectful as possible, Seb struggled to hold everything in check. His wolf didn't like Jason talking about her, and the mention of vampires being near here was too much. It paced within him, hackles up, and as he swallowed he felt his throat work, the growl forcing its way out.

His forearms tensed, and his fingers ached as his grip tensed around her delicate hand.

The shocked gasp from Jess had him whipping his gaze to her, sure that he'd hurt her, only to find her staring, stunned, at his hands.

Dark, deadly looking claws tipped his fingers, and he instantly let her go, pulling away from her. "Jess, I—"

Her eyes shone lavender as she slowly reached out, taking his hand back, lacing their fingers together. "You won't hurt me."

The rage and wild anger raced away in a rush, leaving fear and doubt in their place. "You don't know that."

Leaning forward to get a better look at his hands, Jason laid his own palm flat on the table, releasing his claws with a sibilant hiss. They looked like his own hands just had, and Seb raised his eyes to Jason.

"She's right, Seb. You won't hurt her, ever. Your wolf won't let you." Rising from the table, he retracted his claws, picking up their bowls.

Placing them in the sink of the open plan kitchen, he stared back at them both as he leant on the breakfast bar. "But the next few hours are going to be tough on you. On both of you."

Not even sure he wanted to hear the answer, he asked anyway. "Why?"

"The full moon is tonight. The first physical change is always brought on by the full moon, which is also why your wolf is so close to the surface. After that, you'll be able to shift at will. But for now, the wolf just wants out."

Releasing his hand, Jess stood up, pacing to the patio doors, staring out at the ocean. "And how do we keep the wolf calm in the meantime?"

~

WANDERING THROUGH THE QUIET VILLAGE, Jess looked up at him as they walked, fighting the urge to grin. Apparently the wolf was inquisitive, and liked new things to look at. He also liked fresh air and the outdoors.

So she and Jason had decided a walk would help.

The row of shops faced the ocean, and as the tide rolled back in, it brought the wind with it. The sun was dropping below the edge of the horizon, leaving the daytime behind, and Jess pulled up her hood as the chill caught her ears, making her shiver.

"You're cold; we should go back. This is a daft idea, anyway. You may as well have put a collar and lead on me."

Unable to keep the humor from her voice, she took his

hand, the raw warmth of him sinking into her skin. "Don't worry, you're quite safe; I don't go for that sort of thing."

Arching a flat stare at her, he rolled his eyes, trying to smoother a smirk.

"Besides, it's just a bit chilly. I'm an islander. We know wind and freezing rain, believe me."

Despite the chill, the fair at the far end of the promenade had begun switching on its lights, and she gave him a little nudge. "Would your friend like to have a look round the fair?" She gave him a winning smile, laughing when he nudged her back...

"No, *he* most definitely would not. Why are you so cheerful, anyway? You're out here, in the freezing bloody cold, having to take me for my evening *walk*."

Much preferring his grouchy mood to the fear and uncertainty they had been facing, she leaned into him. "I'm happy. I'm worried and nervous, for sure. But I'm also happy. You're not a vampire, and I didn't have to make a life-changing decision about a dear friend." Waiting for the lone car on the road to drive past, she pulled him towards the beach.

The lights from the boats bobbed about in the distance, and the music from the fairground carried softly when the wind blew in their direction.

Coming to a standstill at the sea wall, he pulled her hand into the pocket of the coat he'd taken from Jason, warming her. "Why are you worried?"

Continuing to stare out across the waves, she let the salty air push against her hood, blowing it down. It whipped through her hair, blowing it up, making her wish she could lift into it. "Let's get through the next twenty-four hours, and we'll worry about my worries after that."

Jason had explained a great deal as the afternoon had passed, but it was what he wasn't saying that concerned Jess. Seb's wolf was so close to the surface, that Jason had decided it'd be safer if they waited until after he'd made his first change, before they talked about anything that involved *matehood*.

And as Seb's wolf wouldn't be able to cope with her going somewhere alone with Jason, she couldn't even get the answers herself.

And in all honesty, she wasn't sure she was ready to hear them, anyway.

"It's about you being my mate, isn't it?" The quiet certainty of his voice sent panic skittering across her skin.

It wasn't fair on him to talk about this now, he had enough to cope with; the moon would begin to rise soon. And she couldn't even let herself think about the cycle of what was going to happen. "Seb. We'll talk about it all. After."

He turned his back to the sea, leaning against the wall, the blue of his wolf ringed his brown eyes. "No. I understand what this means. My wolf has recognized you as his, but that doesn't mean it's the same for you." His wolf eyes bled into the brown. It was as if he was trying to rationalize with the preternatural creature that lived within him.

And he was having none of it.

His breathing deepened, taking on a chuffing quality that had her looking at her watch. The moonrise began at 7.42—in just over an hour. "Sebastian." Cupping his jaw in her palms, she lifted his face, happy to see the wild blue of his gaze slowly receding as she ran her fingers through his hair. Stroking the nape of his neck, she stepped into his embrace. "The wolf may want one thing, but you also get to choose. And I'm here right now, so let's get through tonight."

As he opened his mouth to protest she laid her lips over his, loving the way his arms came instantly and fully around her, wrapping her against him. She'd meant for the kiss to be soft, to gently offer comfort. But as her fingernails lightly

163

scraped his scalp, he groaned. The strength of his embrace briefly chased away thoughts of what was to come.

His lips demanded her supplication, his searching tongue ravaged her mouth. He stroked boldly over her, palming her ass with a heavy hand.

She caught her breath at the assault on her senses, the intensity of her reaction to him. Her body readied for his in a rush, and she sighed, wanting to get closer. She traced the heavy shadow across his jaw, moaning as he took her bottom lip between his, stroking his tongue across the sensitive flesh.

Standing between his spread legs, she leaned heavily onto him, savoring the hard pressure of his shaft. His fingers kneading her ass, pulling her into him, left her panting, and she pulled briefly away to catch her breath.

Groaning, Sebastian buried his head against her chest, her warm coat becoming a barrier, keeping him from her luscious breasts.

As a gull arced overhead, its piercing cry echoed over the waves as it soared, she let her head hang back, her hair swaying as she watched the bird. The first stars were slowly waking, and as she shifted her fingers through his hair, she held him to her.

Her desire subsided at the sight of each new star, and whispering his name, she looked into his interchanging eyes.

"We'd better get back."

Reluctantly stepping away from him, she held out her hand, waiting for him to take it.

Their silence deepened with each step of the short walk back to her home, the gravity of the approaching moon weighing heavily.

The soft white street lights shone hazily as mist travelled in on the tide, and the closer they got the tighter the ball in her stomach became.

She loved the Halloween season, carved jack-o-lanterns sitting on most doorsteps, their candles flickering.

As they walked past the closed farm shop, a trailer loaded with pumpkins of every shape and size stood on the forecourt, ready for the weekend's carving fair.

She smiled wistfully at the 'Everyone Welcome' sign, with a plethora of plastic bats and spiders hanging from it.

She'd hadn't given a thought to Samhain this year, hadn't begun her usual ritual of leaving gifts for the spirits.

Turning onto her little road, the branches of the cherry trees had shed their leaves, the autumn winds were chasing them around their feet.

One of her neighbors was just getting home from work, and Jess murmured a quiet 'good evening' as they passed by.

Everything seemed so normal, so normal it felt impossible to think that in a couple of hours her lover would make his first full body shift into the shape of his wolf. A wolf that recognized her as his own.

Jason stood at the open front door, a coffee in his hand, leaning against the door-jamb. His face pensive as they approached.

Letting them walk on indoors, she hung their coats up, taking a minute to look at herself in the hallway mirror. Worried brown eyes looked back her; she wasn't used to having to totally surrender control.

Placing her palm on the mirror, she pooled magic in the glass. As she watched it shimmer like water beneath her hand she whispered a plea to the spirits to keep him safe. Clenching her fist, she pushed the request into the glass, letting it go, out into the ether.

Following after them, she stopped at the doorway, her furniture had all been moved, pushed as best as possible into one corner, stacked together.

Jason came to her side, giving her shoulder a squeeze at

her undoubtedly shocked expression. "He's going to need space, and I'd like to protect your things." His voice trailed away at Seb's low growl.

Jason turned to face his friend, and Jess's breath hitched at the sight of his wolf eyes. They'd completely eclipsed the brown, and were focused on Jason's hand on her shoulder.

Bristling, Jess readied herself to let her mouth operate without the help of her brain, when Jason slowly shook his head, carefully lifting his hand from her.

"Seb, Jess is my friend." His voice was deliberately calm as he spoke. "I don't want her to have deal with any carnage—and neither do you."

His head reared back, wolf-like, as he processed Jason's words, before looking at Jess. "No. No, I--I don't want to do any damage." Rubbing his temple, he drew his brows together. "Will I?"

Able to give him nothing more than a shrug, Jason turned to Jess. "Can you put a protection spell up? Something that will keep all prying eyes out and dampen the noise, that sort of thing?"

Raising her hands with a nod, she was just about to chant when Jason stopped her.

"Can you put a perimeter on the boundary, too? He shouldn't go anywhere, but let's make sure."

Tailoring her protection spell, she began to chant.

Both Jason and Seb looked uneasily around them as the magic rose, the power of the gathering spirits filling the room with static pressure.

As she reached her final repetition, power seethed around her.

A snapping sound echoed through the house, leaving Jess raising her brows. She'd put more mojo into this incantation, but it would seem the spirits were also lending an extra hand with the cloaking aspect of the spell, leaving old energy thrumming all around.

"We're safe."

Seb was standing, his hands braced on the side as he stared out of the kitchen window, towards the dark beach.

Crossing to him, she touched his arm, noticing the fine sheen of sweat that covered his brow. "You okay?"

"I'm sure I've had worse days."

Chuckling lightly at his black humor, she stroked down his arm, taking his hand.

Jason's hushed voice reached them. "It's almost time." He'd been standing in front of the patio doors, staring out into the night.

Looking at them, he crossed his arms over his chest, his face set in hard lines. "Jess, I want you to go into the bedroom and close the door."

Whirling to face him, she planted her hands on her hips, her response instant. "I will not."

"There's no argument in this, Jess. His change will be... difficult, and if you get upset or try to help, his wolf will do everything it can to try and give you what you want. The change could take *days* instead of hours." Ruffling his hair back from his face, he threw his hands out. "Is that what you want?"

Her argument died, fear and panic ripping through her. This was really going to happen, and there was nothing she could do. On a whispered breath, she hung her head. "No."

Jason's shoulders sagged in relief, and in a moment of guilty clarity she saw how tired he was. Exhaustion sat heavy on him. She'd been so busy worrying about Sebastian, then about herself, she hadn't once wondered about him.

He must've been beside himself at the thought the vampires had taken them...

Shame dropped through her at what she'd put him

through. "Jason, I'm so sorry."

As she rushed towards him, he held up his hands. Throwing her an awkward smile, he warded her off. "Let's not piss off the pup, Sweetheart. Give me a hug tomorrow."

She stopped in her tracks, suddenly aware of the seething energy pouring off Seb.

Taking a moment, she drew in a breath.

She stood between them, with Seb's jealousy filling the room like an entity. His lingering growl grew louder, as his claws extended, and he stepped towards Jason, his eyes completely eclipsed by the blue of his wolf.

It was one thing for her to make allowances because of tonight, but would she always be expected to step back? Would she be expected to continuily behave in ways that worked for him? Cutting herself of from friends, from giving affection?

Turning stark eyes from Seb, she looked to Jason. "Is this how it is now? I'll be expected to check my behavior, my every action, to allay the wrath of the beast?"

A pained expression crossed Jason's face, as he shook his head at her, his voice gentle as his eyes beseeched her. "Jess. There's so much more to explain, but now isn't the time."

She knew she was wrong, but the words didn't seem to stop falling. The panic was absolute, gripping her. "It is, isn't it?! I've become chattel. Is this what is to be the mate of wolf?"

Jason's eyes pooled blue, as his rough whisper reached her. "So I've been told."

Seb gripped her arm, wrenching her round to face him. His blue eyes furious as he pulled her to him. "Don't ever turn to another over me." His wolf ruled him now, even altering the depth of his voice. She had no time to react as she crashed into his body. His lips were hard and punishing as they took hers, and as she struggled against him he locked her in his embrace. Trapping her. Keeping her where he wanted.

Fury ripped through her, to match that of any wolf, as magic toiled from her palms. Fighting until she could lay her hands on him, she shot him across the room. Lavender static still hazing around her as he hit the floor.

Magic, ancient and welcome, raced through her as he came to his feet. His expression stunned as he faced her, the wolf and the man shocked by her actions. "Jess…"

"I do as I please!" Her voice rang out as she stared him down. Catching Jason poised, standing to the side of her, he was clearly ready to throw himself into the melee if needed, although she wasn't sure whose side he'd by on.

Sebastian still looked shell shocked, as if the throw had winded him.

Scraping back his hair, he looked at her, what he'd been about to say lost as he doubled over.

Fear erupted, outweighing the riot of emotion pouring through her, as she ran to him, trying to take his weight.

Sebastian gripped her, his body hot as if riddled with fever as he pulled back, away from her, a groan wrenched from him. "Please, Jess, just go, don't see me… Jase, get her out."

Seb's palms hit the wooden floor with a thump, as Jason's gripped her upper arms, and she allowed him to hurry her along the hallway.

Opening the door to her room, he backed her inside, his eyes shadowed with worry as they focused on her.

"It's gonna be bad, Jess, there's no point in hiding it. But do not come out."

Closing eyes that were filling with tears, she blinked them away, and lifted her chin. "Take care of him."

She closed the bedroom door on her friend, waiting until she heard his footsteps walking away before pulling in great gasping breaths, fighting back the burning tears.

CHAPTER 12

PROPPING her bedroom window open wide, she knelt on the bed, her arms crossed over as she leant on the sill.

The sea and the darkness blew over her face as she looked out into the cold October night, watching the full Hunter Moon fill the sky.

She'd been in here for hours; she'd paced until there was no floor left, and all that had reached her was silence, littered with occasional dampened voices from her front room.

But as the moon rose higher in the sky, tension knotted within her.

As the witching hour approached, small sounds began to filter in. Jason's calm voice seemed to whisper down the hall, as the discord rose.

She held stock-still, her eyes closed as the bedlam took hold. She didn't flinch or jump as something crashed to the floor, as the energy pounded and breathed, pushing against her metaphysical boundaries, bowing them out.

She held her stillness through the groaning, biting her lips at the horrendous noise of bones altering, and skin tearing.

But as a low keening cry lit the air, she couldn't hold back the tears.

They streamed like hot rivers down her cheeks, as she held back any sound. Until, finally, it all stopped.

The cold air cooled her burning face, as a heavy silence rang out, chilling her to the bone. The silence went on and on, until she couldn't stand it any longer.

Launching herself from the bed, she flew across the room.

Halting, she stared at her trembling hand wrapped around the doorknob, as her feet softly touched the floor. She listened for any hint of noise.

The silence was broken as an unearthly howl rent the night, and gasping, she stumbled back, her heart pounding in her chest.

Jason's relieved laugh sounded, and as the back of her legs hit the bed she sat down. What could possibly be funny?

Panting echoed along the hallway, accompanied by the sound of claws on hardwood.

"Holy-shit. Dammit, Seb, will you hold on—"

Jason was trying to explain something, and at the sound of a loud thump and Jason's curse, she jerked her head towards the door.

Long, heavy breaths sounded loudly through the wood, and she sat for a moment, unsure if she was terrified.

Placing a hand over her pounding heart, she focused on the door, wondering what was on the other side. Was Seb still there, or did he have to hand over to the wolf?

As she sat, she wondered why he wasn't simply bursting into the room. But as wisps of sadness reached her, she came to her feet. He was afraid; afraid she wouldn't accept him.

Placing her hand back on the doorknob, it didn't tremble this time, and as she pulled the door open, her eyes widened in shock.

A fully-formed wolf stood before her, his caramel fur the

same color as Seb's hair. He was enormous, tail hanging low, his ears slightly dipped.

A few feet was all that lay between them.

Unsure what to do, she knelt slowly, her palms on her thighs, rubbing against the soft denim of her black jeans.

His head still low, he took a tentative step closer, the heavy panting easing. Another step brought him close enough to nudge her hand with his muzzle.

Ever so softly, she touched his chest, encouraging him with tender words to lift his face, to look at her.

The eyes of his wolf, so searingly blue, were mixed with her Sebastian's eyes, and they both looked at her, wracked with doubt that she would turn them away.

Caressing his face with her hand, she smiled. "Sebastian." Certainty filling her. "It's still you."

Dropping his head, he pushed his forehead to her chest, the maple of his fur a sharp contrast to her silky black top.

Sliding her hands into his ruff, a small watery giggle escaped her lips as she smoothed her face against his fur, and relief swept through her like a fresh tide.

Her hair dropped across her shoulder as she touched her forehead to his, nuzzling him in return.

His shape subtly shifted beneath her hands, and the wolf began to flow away. The bulk of the beast faded, leaving Seb's strong smooth shoulders and ruffled hair.

The small click of the front door announced Jason's departure, and she made a mental note to buy her best friend the best bottle of Scotch in existence.

But later. She'd do that later.

With a final flex of his hands, his claws retracted and Sebastian sat before her, hair hanging in eyes that contained both wolf and man, and she couldn't help another giggle as she cast her eyes

down. "You're naked."

Trying to say her name, he tested his voice again before finally speaking with a lopsided smile. "Did you expect me to shift back fully dressed?"

Not giving her chance to answer, he cupped the back of her neck, pulling her to him, his lips searching as they pressed against hers.

Cupping her jaw in his hands, he eased her head back, looking into her eyes. "It's not just the wolf in me that knows you. You're ours. Mine *and* his." Halting briefly, he seemed to search for the words. "But we don't own you, and you won't have to pacify him. Or me, for that matter." A tired chuckle left his lips. "You can just taze us with one of those ear-ringing electricity bolts if we get out of line."

Touching her soft cheek, his expression earnest as he held her gaze. "I love you, Jess."

Her bottom lip trembled as he spoke, and her heart swelled with myriad emotions as she sat on the floor in her hallway. "I don't think me tazing you is something we want to make a habit of."

Reaching out, she stroked him, his arms, shoulders, across his chest. "And I love you."

Needing to be near him, she touched her lips to his, moaning at his deep earthy taste, not understanding why he pulled back, catching her wrists, stopping her from touching him.

"You need to be sure, Jess. Things are different now that my wolf is...here. He has needs, too."

Clearing her throat, arousal trickled through her, as she wondered what *he* might want. "Like what?"

His eyes fired blue as he looked at her, his grip tightening around her wrists, a slightly dazed look crossing his face.

"Sebastian? Like what?" Her breaths shortened as he stared at her, his thumbs rubbing over her pulse points, as he slowly leaned towards her, his lips almost touching hers when he spoke.

"Your eyes, they've changed." A low growl rumbled from him as he placed his lips ever so softly just beneath her ear, his hot breath sending shivers up spine. "What would you like from us?"

Her head dropped back as he spoke. Holding her wrists in one hand, his rough fingers tucked her hair behind her ear, smoothing it away from her throat.

She held her breath as he dragged his kiss down her neck. Desire pooled low in her belly. She ached for him, her body readied, and she waited, hoping she wouldn't need to spell it out...

A high whimper left her lips as she felt the scrape of his fangs. She knew they were longer, sharper now. And she moaned, pressing closer to their deadly length.

His growl was deeper as he laved her neck, vibrating through her, leaving her bereft when he pulled away.

"Nooo..." Opening heavy-lidded eyes, she looked up at him. His were lit with an unearthly glow, and his lethal fangs were breath-taking to her.

"Jess," his voice was a harsh rasp of sound, "do you want my bite?"

She clenched her hands to fists in his grasp, as she grew wetter in a rush. She shook her head, sending her hair rippling around her shoulders, trying to clear the fog, trying to think; she knew that a bite from a werewolf could turn her. But she also knew a bite between mates would link them, giving them a lifelong metaphysical connection.

Was she ready for a lifetime?

Her voice was nothing more than a feathered whisper when she spoke. "Can I?"

Groaning, he shook his head hard, briefly looking upwards. "Woman, you test me."

As she watched him a sheen of sweat covered his chest, and she fought the urge to lick him.

"You'd be mine, Jess. Do you understand? He and I crave it. But a mate-bite will bind us."

Seb's face was so serious as he looked at her, and his hand trembled slightly as he ran his finger along her jaw. It all became clear in rush; it wasn't whether she was ready for a lifetime, but if she could live her life without him.

She let his words sink through her before she said, "I'm already yours."

At her words, he lifted her hands, placing them over her breasts, the silk of her shirt rubbing beneath her palms.

"Then lose the clothes."

A slow smiled teased her lips as her palms crackled with magic, until she sat naked before him, cupping her breasts.

Grasping her waist, he lifted her over him, sitting her in his lap as she wrapped her long, beautiful legs around him.

Twinning her arms around his shoulders she could feel the heat of him, pressing up between her spread thighs. His hands cupped her buttocks, taking her weight as he slowly rubbed his chest across her breasts.

She wriggled in his grasp, desperate to feel him inside, and pressed fully against him, soaking up his heat.

His fingers kneaded her soft flesh, as he slowly lowered her.

The heavy head of his shaft pushed into her slick depths, and she clenched around him as he held her there. Her muscles fluttering. Gripping and moving. Wrenching heavy moans from both of them.

Letting his palms slide over her and up her back, her weight flowed down, taking him in, in one sweet, long motion.

Catching her breath, she arched, holding still, knowing she was already close, just wanting to hold on a little longer.

But his hands settled on her hips, gripping her, jerking her down, grinding her onto his length, she knew it was too late. Jess moved with the rhythm he set, biting her lip, as each roll of her hips brought her closer.

His kiss was carnal and deep as he took her mouth, his hands brushing up her throat, sweeping her hair aside, holding her where he needed her.

Involuntary cries left her lips as his fangs teased her and her legs gripped him as she fought the all-consuming need to come.

Grabbing her hips once again, he held her still. Packed tight within her.

Her cries became begging whispers as he licked her skin, readying her, as she tried to move. His breath panted against her, his fingers digging into her flesh as he slowly circled her hips.

"Come for me."

As his words reached her, his fangs pierced her skin, the pain and pleasure a perfect mix as she crashed over the edge.

Undulating against him, his heavy growl reverberated through her, intensifying her delight.

His shaft throbbed within her, as he pulled his fangs free, his growl becoming a moan as he came.

She pushed down, taking as much of him as she could. Wanting to feel his every pulse as her orgasm ebbed away.

Struggling to open her eyes, she watched him, as his head dropped back.

Wild color flashed across his cheekbones, his mouth slightly parted, and she knew the sight of her blood on the tips of his fangs would be an image she'd take out and play with. Again and again.

As his breathing eased, his heavy-lidded gaze fastened on her. "Were you watching me?"

Tracing her finger down the center of his chest she merely smiled at him. "Yes."

Chuckling beneath his breath, he patted her ass. "Can't argue with that."

Trying to untangle herself from him, she slowly came to her feet, holding her hand out, pulling him up. "Come to bed."

~

THE MOTORWAY WAS long behind him as Jason drove. The full beams on the low slung Mercedes sliced through the darkness, catching the stunned gazes of a herd of fallow deer, as he sped through the southern countryside.

His relief at seeing Jess put Seb and his beast in their place still sat with him. But not enough to relieve the dread of the task ahead.

The road thinned the further he drove, there were no streetlights or road markings, but it didn't matter to him. He knew these roads too well. Had hoped he'd never come back here.

The tiny chapel rested at the top of a steep incline. It had no resident priest or parish.

It was widely believed that the village it served had been wiped out by plague in the sixteen hundreds, but Jason knew better.

Turning off the headlights, the Mercedes purred as she climbed, her tires crunching as she rolled across the gavel, coming to a stop at All Hallows Church.

Cutting the engine, he sat, letting the complete silence of the night surround him. The full hunter moon bathed the hillside in pearly light, and Jason would have liked nothing better than to shift and run with the night.

But it wasn't to be.

Pulling his phone from his pocket, he texted Jess.

Even though you've been at home more than you've been at worker,
(slacker)
Seb needs a couple of weeks off, to adjust.
I'm sure you'll want to help him with that.
I'll let you know when we need to be back at the desk.
J x

Dropping his phone on the passenger seat, he unfolded his frame from the car.

Drawing the medieval key from his pocket, he grasped the door, not surprised to find it already unlocked.

His senses rioted as he crossed the threshold. The nearly empty church was eerily still, the moon striking the stained glass windows, catching the centuries of different strains of Christianity, reflecting the colors across the plain stone walls.

Walking up the aisle, his eyes peered into the shadowy corners until he found her.

Her small frame was no reason to judge her as helpless, this he knew too well. The heavy sweep of her bright red hair was a fine mark of her Irish heritage, and was nowhere near enough of a warning for her wrathful temper.

And despite having experienced her temper and her magic, many times, he was just too tired to be careful.

"Why, Lucy O'Leary? What the bloody-hell are you doing here?"

EPILOGUE

TWO WEEKS LATER

"MARRIED?!" Thea launched from her open front door, wrapping her sister up in her embrace. "When? How long have we got to plan? Ohmygods, Jess, you're getting married!"

Slamming the car door, Adam walked down Thea's drive, eyeing his over-excited sister.

"Who's getting married?"

Despite the joyful commotion, the freezing November morning still left Jess stifling a shiver, as she laughed, lifting her hand.

The ring was ornate gold. Seb had chosen sapphire for the sea, and Jess couldn't help but catch her breath every time she looked at it.

Eyeing the ring, Adam turned to Seb. "You work fast."

Shrugging off what Seb knew was brotherly concern, he looked at Adam. "Don't want to waste a minute."

Marc came up behind Thea, looking at the unexpected family gathering on their drive.

"You lot going to stand out there, or you coming in? It's bloody freezing."

"They're getting married!" Thea smiled joyfully up at Marc. "Can you believe it?" Too excited to give him time to answer, she whipped back round to Jess. "When?! What date have you picked?"

Knowing Thea was going to panic, Jess gave her a winning smile before saying, "Well, we thought Christmas Eve."

All eyes turned to them, as Seb wrapped his arm around Jess's waist. "And we thought we'd do it down here, on the Island."

Thea placed her hand on her heart, laughing nervously. "You mean Christmas Eve next year..." She nodded encouragingly at Jess, who merely shook her head.

"Nope."

"Lordy, we've got a lot to do." Grabbing Jess's hand, she pulled her free from her future husband, dragging her into the house. "Come on. And you lot too, don't dawdle. Lots to do!"

Jess threw a plea for help over her shoulder, but Seb shrugged, giving her a wink, before turning to the two men who would soon be his family. Sliding his hand inside his coat, he produced a bottle of Glenmorangie 1983. "Shouldn't we at least have a drink to celebrate?"

Slapping him on the back, Adam laughed, getting an approving nod from Marc, as Murphy pushed through their legs, making his way into the warm. "Welcome to the mad house."

The End

COLD MOON

Read Chapter One of *Cold Moon*, the next book in the series!

CHAPTER 1

OCTOBER (2017)

THE LOW VIBRATION in his pocket had him reaching for his phone.

Adam stared down at the screen: no caller ID.

"Hello?"

"Well now, and isn't that a voice to bring a smile to my face."

The rhythmic Irish brogue dropped through him like a dead weight.

"Dillon." Adam didn't bother asking how he'd got this number, or what he wanted.

He'd known Dillon would turn up eventually. He'd just hoped that eventually would turn into a few decades.

"Adam. So you're back in the bay, and been there for a while, I gather. You know, I didn't figure you for the home-body type."

The veiled malice crawled across him, leaving an almost tangible layer of grime on his skin.

"We all change. What do you want?" He

deliberately kept his voice even and calm. He could feel Dillon tapping at the edges of his energetic field, seeing if there were any cracks in his armour, if there was any way in.

He was careful to keep his rage banked, not wanting to give Dillon anything to draw out, anything to latch on to.

"Want? Why, I don't want anything, boyo." Wretched glee dripped from each word. "But you see, I'm in London. Doing a bit of a protection favour for a friend, so I am. You see, his normal witch was busy, she'd had to fly off. To Greece of all places. Now he's got a real problem, this friend of mine, needed his mojo all topped up. And there I am, doing my thing, and imagine my surprise when I pick up the distinct traces of Lavelle magic. Naturally I'd recognise it."

Adam's grip on the phone tightened with each word, the tension across his shoulders pooling, burning a red-hot trail down his spine. He gritted his teeth against the pain, giving Murphy a fierce look. Warning him to stay where he was, he opened the patio door, and stepped out.

Leaving Murphy safely shut inside the house, he headed for the steps that lead down to the ocean. He gritted his teeth against the frustration caused by the leg brace, but he had no choice but to drag himself to the sea. He knew the banked rage and anger was going to come pouring out, nothing could stop it.

The bitterly cold night brought no relief to his searing skin, from the heat bubbling up from the core of him.

"And you know, boyo, it occurred to me; I surely hope that my friend's problem doesn't come looking for your sister."

The line went dead, and Adam dropped the phone to the pebbles. He was powerless, he couldn't even walk properly!

Yanking his hoodie over his head, he hobbled towards the frigid ocean.

The skin on his hips and across the base of his spine tore and stretched as he pushed the cargo shorts away, molten lava bled from within him, ignited by rage, and he couldn't help but yell out as a salty wave hit him. Hissing as it made contact.

The sound was lost to the water as he plunged into its depths. He gave his agonised shouts to the swirling sea, letting the icy depths cool the torturous burning.

Flames licked through his veins, illuminating the water as he swam deeper. Knowing the sea was the only thing that could stop the uncontrollable fire consuming him.

Dillon shut down the mobile, dropping it on the covers. He let his tired body ease down to the plushly-made bed.

Sitting, he stared into the long mirror in front of him. The overtly lavish hotel room fanned out in the reflection. His bare feet were cushioned in the deep carpet, the wall of windows opposite looked out over London. The lights from the London Eye reflected up, from the water of the Thames.

He couldn't afford the hotel suite, but as he stared at himself in the mirror, he watched a small smile lift the edges of his mouth.

"Whether I can afford it or not, don't matter now."

His Irish lineage was obvious, thick red hair, blue eyes, pale skin. His time in Dublin had tainted his southern Irish roots, but he was what he had always been; a witch of the old country.

"And for once, I'd better not let my kin down."

After fifty-three hours of no sleep, his body had become nothing more than one moaning ache, but ignoring the call of the big bed, he pushed to his feet.

Sitting down at the dresser, he slid the mahogany leather desk blotter in front of him. Squaring it up, he placed the pen to the right side, and laid the envelopes above. It was pleasing to him, and he may as well enjoy things that pleased him.

The thick hotel stationary felt good and right beneath his hand, and the smooth noise of the round-nibbed fountain pen calmed his thoughts as he began to write.

He made sure to say sorry for being a royal pain the arse, made sure to ask her to take white tulips to their mother's grave on her birthday, made sure to explain what he'd done.

Laying the pen down, he straightened up, arching the kinks from his spine. He shuffled the two pages together, folding them neatly.

He scrunched his nose at the sharp taste of the seal on the envelope. He'd been five, sat next to his mother on the grass, and she'd helped him write a letter to his grandparents, shown him how to mark a kiss, write the address, where to put the stamp.

He let the bittersweet memory wash over him.

Making the call to room service he requested they come and take the letter.

Holding his hand above it, his low whisper filled the room, his hand shook as magic hazed and the protection spell was complete, and he gloried in the feeling of power. The same as he always had.

The knock on the door had him lifting his head, once-again catching his gaze in the mirror.

"Well, boyo, here we go."

Placing his hand on the crystal doorknob, he felt the power tremor beneath his palms. Once he opened the door the seal would be broken.

"And now's as good a time as any."

Pulling it open, he gave the bellhop a warm Irish smile. "Why thank you, laddie. This letter is for my sister." Placing the letter and a twenty pound note on the tray, he made sure to look the young man straight in the eye. "I want you to see to it, that this gets in the post straightway."

With the courteous response still hanging in the air,

Dillon shut the door. As the latch clicked shut a different kind of energy filled the suite.

The long heavy voiles on the windows moved as if caught in a breeze, and the lights flickered and sparked.

Never one to shy away from anything, he drew the curtains as far open as he could, letting in all of the London skyline, before sliding open the large bi-fold doors, welcoming the rainy night.

The sound of the street rose up from below, and he fought a moment of sadness; he loved life. Loved every nuanced moment, but it was fair to say that he'd lived it in a fit of revelry. And he'd be damned if he didn't go out the same way.

"It's no good *hanging* about out there, I let my own protection spell down, so you may as well come in."

Crossing his arms over his chest, he made sure to notice the feel of the fine silk shirt against skin. If he was going out, then by-the-Goddess he was doing it in style.

The tall elegant blonde traced before his eyes, taking form in front of him. Gods', she was lovely.

"You know, it has me wondering, how anything as beautifully packaged as you are, could be so bloody evil."

Her laugh was lilting as she stepped over the threshold. The lights caught the thick, gold slave bangles that wrapped around her upper arms, and her skin had a warm beachy hue, that made her look hot to the touch.

But he knew better.

"Evil is just a word, Cherie. A word created by man, to make other men afraid of a non-existent god." She walked around the suite, touching the fabrics and furniture, stroking the bed. "But then, you also consider yourself evil, do you not?"

Her French accent brought a strange beauty to her words, and the smile he gave her was laced with genuine humour. "Aye, I used to think so. If only I'd met you sooner, I could've put all that behind me. But that's living for you. It is what it is."

As she stopped before him, he found he was pleased, masochistically speaking, to find that his last moments were going to be denying the wants of this truly spectacular creature.

"So, mon Cher, I need the barriers on the museum dropped, and I'd rather you just do it... Than me have to drain every last drop from you, take your memories as my own, and hunt down everyone you know and love." She waved her hand as she spoke, batting away the open threat she'd made.

He smiled into dead eyes, their depths hollow, and waited silently as she studied him, a slight lift to her perfectly shaped lips revealing the deadly tips of her fangs.

"Cherie, I find that you are so much more than I was expecting, maybe you'd prefer I work it out of you another way, non? But you should know, I like to keep my pets." She paused a beat before adding. "So, Dillon O'Leary, of the Clan O'Leary, a hereditary Witch of the Morrigan, what's it going to be?"

Her heated look was enough to convince him that partaking in parlour games with a vampire wasn't for him, and he knew, with certainty, that he'd take death over ever being her play thing.

"*Everyone you know and love*, huh? I'd like to say I don't believe you can do that, but sadly, I know better. And I've wondered for a while if that's how your scourge was slowly creeping back." Deadly rage crawled across her face at his insult, but he merely continued to speak. He'd made his peace, this was where he made his stand. "So here's the deal. I'll drop the barriers. But only for five of you. In the spirit of fairness and all that."

Her smile had a confused edge as she stared at him, the

lengthening of viscous fangs looked erotically right against her lush, red lips.

He said nothing else as she continued to hold him with her gaze, until all pretence of patience was lost.

With a hiss she whirled away, clicking her fingers as she did so.

The chill at his back told him she'd called for another, and in the milliseconds before he could react a smooth feminine hand slid across his throat, to hold his jaw.

Sharp talons dug into his skin, as even sharper teeth scraped his neck.

The blonde was back, standing before him, as the vampire behind him held him pressed against her freezing body. "I was trying to be reasonable."

Struggling to laugh against the grip at his throat, he rolled his eyes heavenward, before rasping. "Reasonable? I don't think so. Tell me, have you actually got close to the Chalice yet? Or does the wolf make you nervous?"

Her warm brown gaze flooded with red as she lashed out. Her claws rent the silk shirt, and his chest beneath it, and he couldn't stifle the groan of agony.

"Bleed him!"

At her command, fangs pierced his skin. The cold was burning.

A chill crawled through his veins, replacing the warmth of his blood.

She stepped against him, pressing fully into the length of him, slipping her fingers into his hair. "I now own every spell you're working. I know everyone you knew, I know *you*. As if you never existed."

The groan from behind him, told him the deal he'd made was working.

The brunette vampire pushed away, throwing him, stumbling.

He hit the floor, cracking his head. He blinked rapidly.

Her long dark hair, and swirling red eyes came back into focus as she pounced over him, pinning him to the floor. Her claws piercing his skin.

"Make it stop! Make it stop!" Her crazy screams reverberated through his brain, the blood loss and poison leaving him dizzy.

A sharp backhand from the blonde knocked her out of the way, sending her smashing into the opposite wall. The picture and frame crashing to the floor, along with the still rabid vampire.

Yanking him up from the floor, her claws digging in, she seethed.. "What have you done?"

The cold had seeped to his very core. Opening his mouth to speak, he found he couldn't form the words, paralysis leaching into every muscle. The final act of a predator he supposed; to render their prey helpless.

She leant closer, as he tried again, the roiling malevolence in her eyes promising vile retribution if she was displeased.

Grinning drunkenly at her, he relished the thought of it. "I told you, that was the deal."

Dropping him unceremoniously to the floor, she spun to her counterpart. "What's happening?"

"There's nothing! He's empty!" She clutched her head. "Only the museum, only nothing, my head..."

Clearly furious, the blonde scored her skin with her claws, letting the blood run freely. Brushing the dark hair away from the face of her companion, she offered her wrist.

With each draw, the smaller vampire seemed to calm, until finally stepping away with a grateful bow. "Thank you, my Lady."

Dillon slitted his eyes, fighting losing consciousness. He'd wanted to take at least one of them with him, but it wasn't to be. They wouldn't get his memories, or his spells, and he'd called in the cavalry. That would have to be enough.

He longed to hear the chant of distant voices, calling him home. A lone tear escaped, his breath stilling in his lungs. But that would never be.

~

ELLIE YANKED THE STEERING WHEEL, sending her little Mini in a half circle, pebbles spraying across the seafront.

Bolting from the car she ran the length of the beach, stones crunching beneath her soles.

The icy night air stung her face and hurt her lungs as she pumped her arms, running as fast as she could towards Adam's house.

Something was very wrong.

She'd been driving home, barely thinking anything when it had dropped through her; complete, consuming, raw panic. She'd only been halfway across the bridge, leaving the Island, but her pounding heart had her turning the car and racing back.

Adam.

He was hurt.

The sick weight of fear had filled her as she'd sped towards his house.

Ahead of her, his turn of the century house was in darkness.

She gasped at the icy night air hitting her cheeks. But with no time to think about a coat she hurried around the back of his house.

Nothing.

Her ballet flats struggled to find purchase as she went down to the beach.

Dread gnawed at her, and she released a moan of relief as

she caught sight of his silhouette, standing tall, facing out to sea. He was alone, and he was okay; there was still time to reach him.

Digging in, she fought the freezing air burning her lungs, and ran to get to him.

He was throwing something to the ground, before pulling the sweater over his head.

Her hands flew to cover her cry as she stumbled, going to her knees on the stones.

Her wrenching breaths were all she could hear as she watched in horror.

He took an awkward step towards the ocean, the full boot encasing his healing-leg hampering him.

What looked like red-hot embers lit him from within, tracing the length of his spine to seer the skin of his lower back.

Finally naked he pitched forward into the ocean, his yell triggering a whimper from her as she struggled to her feet, staggering towards him.

The sea hissed and heat hazed as he dropped beneath the surface, water bubbling up around him, glowing red and gold.

Her brain had switched into absolute panic mode. Unable to piece together what was happening, she didn't feel the chill of the ocean or the heat of the steam as she waded in after him. Her only thought: his safety.

She was up to her waist, with the seabed slipping away. The waves splashing against her as she frantically reached into the murky depths.

The burning glow was fading, leaving only the dark ocean and even darker night. The cloud hid any hint of the waxing gibbous, Hunter Moon, and her body had begun to shake in reaction with chill and shock.

As she turned full circle she could hear someone calling

his name, and it took precious moments for her to realise it was her. Whispering a litany as she searched for him.

The churning waves calmed around her, as if the seething fury had dispersed from the night air.

He broke the surface, like a demigod born of Poseidon. His auburn hair was longer and thicker than she remembered, and it was plastered around his face, revealing the now golden hue of his once-blue eyes.

He was broad and powerful; could've been carved from marble.

His hands fisted and unfurled as he drew in great heaving breaths, that were visible in the icy night. Before finally closing his eyes, lifting his face to the night sky, letting the newly falling rain soothe him.

"Adam..." His name left her lips once more, as she took a step towards him. Reaching out she was stunned to see the light blue glow of her palms, her need to heal him, to help him, so unbearably intense. "Let me—"

He turned, the move slow and measured. His golden gaze fastened on her. He seemed to be taking her in, studying every inch of her as they booth swayed with the rhythm of the bitter sea.

"Let you... Let you what?"

The short staccato of his words hit like bullets, and she dropped her arms to her sides, self-consciously hiding her hands, letting them hang beneath the surface of the water.

Unable to form words, she shook her head. Not knowing where to begin. Not understanding any of this.

His arms lifted as he spoke, gesturing at his body. "Haven't you done enough to my family—to me?"

Years ago the poisoned hatred of his words would have sent her running. They *had*. She'd holed up to lick her wounds, trying to work through the guilt, trying to make any of it make sense.

But it wasn't years ago, and she'd spent the years since coming to accept that she hadn't done anything wrong. It was far-beyond time that she got to have her say.

Pure, unadulterated anger poured through her as she looked at him.

The clouds had begun to move, letting through slices of the moon's light.

Burns and scars littered his hips, curling around them. But as the ocean lapped at him, each wave healed, until finally only smooth, tanned skin remained.

Planting her hands on her hips, she took a deep, shivering, breath.

Finally.

Finally she was going to have her say.

"What *I've* done? This isn't me, you fool. This is *you*. This is what lives in you." Her voice rose, "I didn't put the magic there. It already existed! Nothing was going to stop that level of power from finding a way out."

She threw her hands wide, shouting out him. "Don't you get it? It was *time!* Even if it hadn't been me, it would still have happened." Her palm hit the water with a slap, her temper flowing full and fierce, in a way she never allowed. She'd put up with his cold ignorance for years, stayed away from her friends; his sister, when he came home. She'd let his deathly apathy push her out. She'd hidden like a scared doe.

Well, no more. No, bloody, more.

"I am so sick of your shit." Her voice rose as the clouds rolled completely away, the pale bands of moonlight laying across them. "You blame me, because that's easy for you, so that you don't have to look any further than me; so you don't have to look at *you*. Well there's so much more to this than you know, and I am so bloody tired of being your whipping boy."

The flat-eyed look she was so used to seeing settled across

his face, and she knew he hadn't heard her. But it didn't matter. He might not understand that she'd crossed a line. But she did; there was no going back.

His voice held a vicious edge as his words reached her. "Well, haven't you grown up. The last time you stuck your nose in where it didn't belong and met my temper you ran away."

Throwing back her shoulders, she lifted her chin, ignoring how the water was numbing her legs and making her bottom lip tremble. "Well, not anymore. My life is here, in the bay—on the Island, and if you're back for good, then you'd better get used to seeing a lot of me. Your sisters and my brother are everything to me, and you won't push me out. I won't let you."

Despite the angry set of his jaw, he seemed to be muttering beneath his breath. Fiery magic hazed in his palms, and with one final glare in her direction, he said, "Then you'd better get used to me, because I'm not going anywhere either."

The waves jerked around him as little flashes of gold sparked the night air, and he disappeared. Leaving wisps of smoke in his wake.

The flash of movement out of the corner of her eye, had her looking up at his house, to see him standing inside—in the warm. The moon bathed the unfairly glorious, naked length of him for a minute, before he turned away.

Her shoulders dropped, any last vestige of energy draining out of her, as freezing shivers wracked her whole body. Shouting at a naked, angry witch, while stood waist deep in the ocean in October, must've been among the top three stupidest things she'd done in this life.

Slowly dragging her freezing body towards the shore, Ellie wrapped her arms around herself, rubbing her chilled skin.

She may be a healer who drew strength from the sea, but she could still end up with bloody hypothermia.

As she made the last few steps from the shallows, teeth chattering and body shivering, she held her hands before her, closing her eyes and placing her palms together.

She drew intense healing warmth from her core, willing the energy down through her legs and up into her arms.

The shivers began to subside, and as she opened her eyes she looked down. No light emanated from her palms. Her healing worked, but with no outside signs, just as it usually did.

The night air picked at her wet clothes, as she trudged the length of the beach, back to her car, still leaving her shivering.

As she looked at her hands, her thoughts wandered to Thea. They had been best friends since Uni, and it'd been over a year before Ellie had worked out that Adam was her brother.

She turned her hands over as she walked, looking at them. She'd never had visible signs of her power, her healing ability had always been something that she had *felt*.

The only times her palms lit-up was when she was with Thea or her sister Jess. And now Adam.

There were so many questions about the connection between their families.

Reaching her Mini, she eased her wet self into the driver's seat, catching her reflection in the review mirror. Her blue eyes stared back at her, and she gave herself a firm nod. "It's time to get some answers."

As soon as Thea and Marc got back from visiting her and Marc's parents in Yorkshire, she'd tell them. Tell them everything; how she'd met Adam, and how all their magic was probably awake because of her. And maybe they could start to figure this thing out.

Adam...

After all these years he still stunned her. Put him within a couple of miles and she felt his pain, she felt *him*. It left her restless and confused. And as ever, drawn to him.

Ellie knew that both Thea and Jess thought Adam shunned all magic from his life. But considering how he'd shifted his form from the ocean to his living room, and the firework display she'd just witnessed, it was clear he was hiding things from all of them. Stopping outside her cottage she turned the engine off, still trying to calm her charged nerves.

They were never going to be able to figure out what the hell all this was about unless everyone was honest, and she very much doubted he'd be inclined to share with her.

Her short mutter lifted to the rolling clouds as she unlocked her front door.

"Well tough."

Adam and Ellie's story, Cold Moon, is widely available. Check out www.joannemallory.com for more details.

ABOUT THE AUTHOR

Joanne Mallory is wife, mother, and canine wrangler. She has always written, everything from poetry to historical papers. But at heart she's always been a romance girl... Romance with a dash of magic.

A history grad, who once managed a castle, she is always finding new things to try and new places to visit.

Joanne was born in Hampshire on the south coast of England, where she still lives with her noisy family, and foolish dogs.

To learn more you can find her at **www. joannemallory.com**

ALSO BY JOANNE MALLORY

THE WITCHES OF LANGSTONE BAY

Thunder Moon

Hunter Moon

Cold Moon

Printed in Great Britain
by Amazon